WITHDRAWN BY THE
UNIVERSITY OF MICHIGAN

A Garland Series
Foundations of the Novel

Representative Early

Eighteenth-Century Fiction

A collection of 100 rare titles
reprinted in photo-facsimile in 71 volumes

Foundations of the Novel

compiled and edited by
Michael F. Shugrue
Secretary for English for the M.L.A.

with New Introductions for each volume by

Michael Shugrue, *City College of C.U.N.Y.*
Malcolm J. Bosse, *City College of C.U.N.Y.*
William Graves, *N.Y. Institute of Technology*
Josephine Grieder, *Rutgers University, Newark*

The Perfidious P---

Anonymous

The Glorious Life and Actions of St. Whigg

Anonymous

The Life and Adventures of Captain John Avery

Anonymous

with a new introduction
for the Garland Edition by
Malcolm J. Bosse

Garland Publishing, Inc., New York & London

1973

820.8
P438
1973

The new introduction for the

Garland *Foundations of the Novel* Edition

is Copyright © 1972, by

Garland Publishing, Inc., New York & London

All Rights Reserved

Library of Congress Cataloging in Publication Data
Main entry under title:

The perfidious P--- (anonymous).

(Foundations of the novel)
Reprint of 3 works, the 1st originally published in London, 1702; the 2d published in London, 1708; and the 3d published in London, 1709.
The life and adventures of Captain John Avery has been attributed to A. v. Broeck.
 1. English fiction--18th century. I. The glorious life and actions of St. Whigg. 1973. II. Broeck, Adrian van. The life and adventures of Captain John Avery. 1973. III. The life and adventures of Captain John Avery. 1973. IV. Series.

PZ1.P415 1973 [PR1297]   823'.5   76-170508
ISBN 0-8240-0518-X

Printed in the United States of America

Introduction

These works represent three important narrative patterns found in the prose literature of early eighteenth-century England: the epistolary novel, the criminal biography, and the scandal chronicle. Of The Perfidious P ———, *Robert Adams Day has written, "technically speaking, it is the best English epistolary novel before* Clarissa.*"*[1] *Like other works of fiction in this literary period,* The Perfidious P ——— *has the explicit moral purpose of warning young girls against "the Practices of a Subtile Man" (p. vi), but in its treatment of an amorous triangle solely through letters, this narrative goes beyond didacticism and achieves an aesthetic success few novels of any kind would attain during the first half of the century.*

The plot turns on Clarinda's inability to prevent the fickle Corydon from shifting his affections away from her. In a short but expert flashback of exposition, Clarinda describes the course of her love affair with Corydon, their happiness, and her romantic notion of their future together. While she is out of town, however, her lover pursues her loyal friend, Lucina, who after much soul searching marries him. Her romantic dreams crushed, Clarinda enters a convent to meditate on her fate. Within the confines of this conventional plot, the author employs the epistolary form for both novelistic

5

INTRODUCTION

and dramatic effects. The continuing innocence with which Clarinda views the burgeoning affair is handled with telling irony, and her eventual helplessness is counterpointed by Lucina's sympathy for her plight. Shifting from one point of view to another, the author makes clear the psychological progress of each character: Corydon's callousness and passion; Lucina's initial loyalty and ultimate perfidy; Clarinda's innocence, desperation, and final calm. The individual style of each letter writer enhances the differentiation of personality.

Lucina expresses herself with an amused objectivity that foreshadows her betrayal of a friend, whereas Clarinda writes of fantasies that emphasize her subjective distance from reality. Having defined character, the anonymous author is able to set in motion the cross purposes and concealment of motives that result in dramatic irony. Often the letters read like speeches in a play, allowing the reader to understand far more than the characters themselves know.

The Perfidious P ——— *is a small but controlled work; variety of technique and psychological clarity compensate for the limitation of its scope. That such a masterful piece of fiction appeared so early in the century is evidence of a creative intelligence working in the epistolary novel long before Samuel Richardson brought the form to fruition in a work of epic length.*

As a forerunner of political satire in the century, The Glorious Life and Actions of St. Whigg *is a burlesque exhibiting some of the virtues and many of the vices of its genre. Written in a zestful, free-wheeling style, it sets*

INTRODUCTION

forth with a bold impudence the partisan attitudes of the day, but vague characterizations and lack of structure tend to blunt the thrusts of its satire. Attacking the Whigs, the Tory author implicates them not only in political chicanery but in religious and sexual offenses as well, implying that villainy is pervasive once it invades the human soul. Consequently, Whigs are accused of being agents both of the Pope and of Calvin. St. Whigg is a hermaphrodite, his mother and sisters are whores, and all his relatives degenerates. In such a broadly conceived polemic, the political insults go beyond Juvenalean indignation and depend for their appeal on their quantity. Aunt Impudence instructs her Whig nephew in the ways of his ancestors, who

> *have been the Plague of Mankind in all Ages, and in whatsoever Countries they have liv'd, have dishonour'd their Maker, Transplanted Peace, Rais'd Discord, Commotions, and Insurrections, Countenanc'd Deism and Impiety, Banish'd Loyalty, Invaded Innocency, Establish'd Schism, and Confirm'd all these where-ever they have erected Commonwealths. (p. 14)*

In comparison to the retrograde Whigs, the exiled James II, for whom the anonymous author is obviously a spokesman, has been changed by experience into a wise and compassionate man. The boldness of the Jacobite defense notwithstanding, St. Whigg *is a crude, defective work which may have served as one of the*

INTRODUCTION

models for Mary Manley's more skillful forays into the genre of political satire.

The Life and Adventures of Captain John Avery, *purportedly written by a Dutchman, is an early tale of piracy and a counterpart to the criminal biographies which dealt with the lives of notorious London characters like Jack Sheppard and Jonathan Wild. The alleged author, Adrian Van Broeck, had reluctantly served as the famous pirate's confidant and amanuensis after being captured off the coast of Java. Promising to describe Avery's career "without assuming to himself any of their [historian] Airs," he supplies the customary background for such biographies, but admirably avoids the mythologizing of young Avery into a childhood monster. In a style more graceful than generally encountered in this genre, the author gives an account of Avery's rise to eminence as a buccaneer, his marriage to a Mogul's daughter, his creation of a pirate empire on Madagascar, his battles on the high seas, and his accumulation of wealth and power. Although Avery's character is barely sketched in, he is judged to be an energetic leader whose "good Genius was superior to his evil." His life seems to be more the reflection of lawless times than of any inherent defect in character, and Avery emerges from these pages as a folk hero who has achieved success through talent and hard work. The account ends abruptly with a short travelog of Madagascar. Although the work is slight, it manages to depict in quiet but firmly constructed prose the balanced*

INTRODUCTION

portrait of a man more ambitious than criminal, more of an empire-builder than a pirate.

Malcolm J. Bosse

NOTE

[1] Told in Letters: Epistolary Fiction before Richardson *(Ann Arbor, 1966), p. 178.*

The Perfidious P---

Anonymous

Bibliographical note:
This facsimile has been made from a copy in the British Museum (12611.ccc.16)

THE
Perfidious P---
BEING
LETTERS
From a
NOBLEMAN
TO
Two Ladies,

Under the Borrow'd Names of *Corydon, Clarinda* & *Lucina.*
With the
Ladies Anſwers.

Printed in the Year, 1702.
Price 1 *s*. 6 *d*.

TO THE

HONOURABLE

Richard Fitz Williams, Esq;

SIR,

I Muſt confeſs I am ſomething at a loſs when I conſider the uſual Method of Dedicators, who when they have finiſh'd their Works, pitch upon a Patron

The Epistle

Patron to whom they may ascribe all the Vertues of their *Hero*; or make him an Instance of all the Perfection and Excellencies of that Piece; by this common Judgment of Dedications, a hasty Reader may be apt to think, I affront my Patron, by engaging him in the defence of a Book wherein I have endeavoured to set off the Baseness and Ingratitude of some Men in their proper Colours; hereby making all

Dedicatory.

all Mankind my Enemies; for Strangers will look upon it as a Satyr leveld at the whole Sex, and my Friends be diffatisfy'd with the Protection of what feems writ againſt themfelves, and ought rather to be laid at the Feet of fome Difconfolate Lady: But the contrary will foon appear, and that 'twas this very Confideration made me pitch upon you, as the only Man whofe Vertues I could oppofe to the Vices of *Corydon*;

The Epistle

don; thereby shewing the World I did not involve the whole Sex in his Guilt; for how many Crimes soever I made him guilty of, I make sufficient amends by giving an Instance of twice as many Vertues in you.

Coridon's Conquests were not rais'd like other Hero's, upon the Foundation, or by force of his Noble Exploits, but rather by the Practices of a Subtile Man upon a Credulous Woman, and the

Dedicatory.

the growth of his Succefs has been influenced only by a feeming Greatnefs, which ferv'd to dazle the Eyes of the weak fighted, and lead them aftray from the Paths of Vertue; but, *Sir,* who ever would perfue thofe Heroick Paths leading to true Honour, need no longer be at a lofs for a Noble Guide, if they know you.

Having thus, in fome meafure, remov'd the Objections that but too readily

The Epistle

ly offer'd themselves against any reception this poor Piece might expect from Men, and given some Reasons for my choosing you in particular, as the most fit Person, whose Noble Generosity might afford a secure Retreat and safe Refuge to the distress'd *Clarinda*, give me leave, *Sir*, to acquaint you also with the Reasons, why above all People in the World, she should find that Protection she desires in you.

'Tis

Dedicatory.

'Tis Title enough to the Protection of a Noble Generous Soul, to stand realy in need of it: The poor *Clarinda* certainly has this Plea, and as for your part, *Sir*, you are not now to be distinguish'd. She was betray'd by a Man Base and Ungrateful, one whose Person, with borrowed Lustre and affected Charms, insnar'd her Heart; but she's now introduc'd to a Man of real Worth, one whose Mind

The Epistle

Mind is illustrated with Vertue, the Beauty and Majesty of which can't so much as be thought of without Love and Veneration: In Short, to recover that good Opinion of Mankind which she lost by *Corydon*, 'tis necessary she be acquainted with you, nor need she fear a cold Reception, where Honour and Affability make their constant Residence.

To

Dedicatory.

To Conclude, *Sir*, in your favourable Entertainment, she is more happy than if she never had been otherwise, and the Goodness you Universally diffuse upon all who have the good Fortune to be near you, can't but sweeten the remainder of her Days, though the Cause of her Grief be never so great. May all Mankind joyn as heartily in contributing what they can to your Happiness, as they do

in

The Epistle, &c.

in a just Admiration of you; and may this, and every new Year, augment the Blessings of the past, which are the Wishes of, *Sir*,

Your most Obedient

Humble Servant,

LETTERS

From a

NOBLE Lord

TO HIS

MISTRESS:

Under the Borrow'd Names of

Corydon and *Clarinda*.

LETTER I.

To *Corydon*.

O Thou Treasure of my Soul! Life of my Life! what shall I call thee? what Epithet find tender enough to express my unequall'd Fond-

Fondness? My poor trembling heart (a young Practitioner in these Affairs, and only taught by you) doubts every Expression, left it want power; or to reveal my Flames, or keep yours ever burning. Be still, thou trusting Flatterer, he will be always mine: he is too Noble, too Generous, to betray; and I am happy, happy above my Sex: One piercing Look or falling Accent from his charming Tongue, gives greater Bliss than all the stupid World can know; one soft hour of melting Love outweighs the Loss of Parents, Family, and Fame.

Oh, my loved Lord, why did the created Powers form thee so divine! each aiding Angel lend a Grace to finish the bright work, and stamp the glorious Heroe supernatural. Oh, I rave! and fixing all my Heaven on thee, my doting Love grows up to Adoration.

You bid me write of my Self, my Health, if I liked my Solitude, and each minute Particular: Alas! how can I descend from Extasies to Trifles fies not worth my care! but you commanded, and I obey. The Place pleafes me as much as I defire to be pleafed when Abfence renders tafte-lefs even the Conveniencies of Life and Joys much more. I fhun all Company, their Affiduities are loft on one fo wrapt in thought as I: my only Queftions are, When the Poft comes in? how often I may fend? Oh write to me, my *Corydon* (for fo I think you gave me leave to call ye) write to me quickly left I grow mad with thinking, left Grief deftroys thofe Charms you have fo often fworn *Clarinda* does poffefs, which I preferve alone for you. Oh give me a Letter that I may read it o'er and o'er a thoufand times, kifs it, blufh at my Folly, put it in my Bofom, and call it You, for I wou'd have it very You. Let it be only Truth, and fure Truth and You are one. What do you do at Court? How pafs your Evenings now after the Duty o'er? Tell me all, be juft like me, and then you never will know when to end.

Oh thofe dying Eyes! at parting, how often has the dear Reflection renewed the killing Tranfports? Well, you love me, I am fure you do; and with that pleafed Thought I leave ye, *Farewel.* Yet I muft go on: Oh love and pity me. Now adieu. Wou'd you had heard that Sigh. *Adieu.*

LET-

LETTER II.

Corydon to *Clarinda.*

Yours, my charming *Clarinda*, I receiv'd at One this Morning, having juſt left my Lord ---- and the Marquis of ---- at the *Rummer*, with whom I drank your Health: The Toaſt was every Man's Inclination, and you was mine by *Jove*; a thouſand times I wiſh'd you preſent, ſo contriv'd, as to appear inviſible to all but me: then I grew uneaſie with my Company, all their Diſcourſes were impertinènt, and each returning Glaſs became as nauſeous as the Embraces of a Woman in the abſence of my lov'd *Clarinda* wou'd be to *Corydon*. Your Letter, my Dear, I read it o'er and o'er, and printed Kiſſes on every Line; and when it bluſh'd, poor Rogue, I hid it in my Boſom, and then methought it whiſper'd, as I remember you ſometimes

times wou'd, *My Life! my Corydon!*

The Devil take Cuſtom; were it not for that, you might be here with me, or I there with you, and no notice taken. Why ſhou'd Generous Souls be fetter'd to the dull Rules of Cuſtom? Nothing but Cuſtom makes a Crime; and Fools are ſtill the moſt cenſorious. A curſe on their prying Curioſity. I can let Tradeſmen cheat, Parſons get drunk, and Wives Cuckold their Husbands, without the leaſt Concern; then why ſhould the buſie World diſturb our Loves? But no matter; I hope a little time will re-inſtate us in our former Tranquillity. I doubt not but when you are known to be in the Country, Fame, who very often errs, will be thought to have bely'd you. I'm ſure if Lovers have any Friends above, your Reputation will be their Care. Oh how I ſhou'd rejoyce to ſee that day when we might hourly meet with frequent Opportunities of renewing our fierce Embraces, when we might give our ſelves over to Loving, nor fear the
watch-

watchful jealous eye. Believe me, *Clarinda*, I have tasted no real Joy since you left me, nor is it possible I shou'd till you return. I'm glad to find you like your Solitude; for that's a friend to Love. My Dear, I cannot tell you how I spend my time, only this, that I'm sure I pass none so pleasantly as that in Writing to you. I am all Extasie when I think on thee, and that's every moment; nay, I break forth in very Poetry:

Oh, in what Raptures did I lately burn!
Now, with what Anguish I your Absence
   mourn!
Think of those Joys, believe these Pains,
   and then,
Forget me, dear Clarinda, *if you can.*
No, thou blest Angel of my Eyes and
   Soul!
  Nothing thy constant Faith can e'er
   remove,
This Thought does ev'ry anxious Doubt
   controul,
  And joins my Heart to thine in bonds
   of mutual Love.

So may juſt Heav'n its Bleſſings deal to me,
As I perform the Vows I've made to thee.

Thus, my Dear, I conclude; and beg you to be content, and reſt as certain of my Love as of the returning Day; and believe, you never ſhall have cauſe to love leſs

Your Faithful

Corydon.

LETTER III.

Clarinda to *Corydon.*

IF after mad Impatiencies, furious Wishes, and wild Desires, when the Blessing is receiv'd I shou'd chide my *Corydon*, wou'd he not think it strange? yet so I must: Your Letter bears too loose a Stile for my Heroick Love; with more Care and greater Study you made your first Approaches to my Virgin-heart. Oh *Corydon!* what a Curse is this on Womankind! Your Dotage is all before a Conquest, Ours begin when you are Bankrupts. How came I to say that, the farthest from my Thoughts? Cou'd I believe thy vast stock of Love does or will receive the least Decay? The bare Apprehension would kill me, and Death's fatal Stroke prevent some greater Ruin.

Remember, *Corydon*, you cannot have forgot it; yet I'll repeat the
pleasing

pleasing Story: The Image always fills my Mind, each Beauty strove to captivate my *Corydon*, and every Dart was aimed at you; my Eyes alone avoided you; I heard your Praises all the Day, your God-like Mein and glorious Actions; I fear'd your Power, and stood upon my Guard; found your Design; for I ne'er look'd up but I beheld you fixt upon my Face; or if you came near in the Crowd, where daily we see each other, how wou'd you sigh! and when by any accident your hand was offered, it trembled so, that I changed Colour too. These were the publick Signs of Love: but oh! at length, with never-ceasing Diligence tracing my Steps with endless Care, *Corydon* found me alone in the Closet of the --- What did you then? Down at my feet the lovely Heroe fell, and cry'd, inhumane Fair, What do you mean by persecuting thus your Slave? If your Resolve is Hate, end with my Life my Sufferings; for whilst I live, I must, I will pursue you with my Love.

Love. Say, *Corydon*, was I not discreet? I broke from thy Arms which graspt my Knees, without one Syllable in answer, and fled to my Companions, who asked me if I had seen a Ghost, my Surprize was such: you followed, saw the pale Confusion, and better skill'd than poor unwary I, made, I fear, a too kind Construction: then, *My Lord*, what pains you took to make a Friendship wherever I did, that I could visit no where but I found my *Corydon*.

This gave you frequent Opportunities; and 'twas at my dear *Lucina*'s Apartments first I heard with patience what you had to say: and oh! when Women listen to the softning Tale of Love, like parlying Towns besieged, they seldom fail the wish'd Surrender.

What am I doing, foolish Creature! Why does this lov'd Remembrance of my past Weakness hang on my Pen? Well, I have done.

Now hear the Difference of our present Lives. You are in the midst
of

of all your Friends, in the midſt of all Diverſions; I baniſh'd from all, knowing no living Creature but my Woman, defiring no Companion but my Book, cheriſhing no Thoughts but thoſe of thee: if I walk, inquiſitive Gazers watch me: then recluſed I never peep abroad, ſuch is my Solitude. But my Love will come and chear me; there's another Hope to ſtrengthen my Courage when I muſt pronounce that melancholly Word *Adieu.*

LETTER IV.

Corydon to *Clarinda.*

WHY all these Doubts and Fears, my Love? Why this needless Repetition? Does my *Clarinda* think I am grown so stupid, so lifeless, for so I must be when I forget the least Particular of what has past between us, those soft Embraces, moaning Sighs and melting Tears, which were too precious to fall unobserv'd, are still fresh in the Memory of *Corydon.* What shall I say more? I think there is nothing more of consequence to say, except I entertain you with Truths obvious to every eye; as, that 'tis Day when the Sun shines, and when he's gone 'tis Night; or, that I love you dearer than all the Women in the World, as great a Truth as either of the former, and ought to be as well known to you. For my part, I think the telling of this over and over, as some Men do their Passions, ought to be tiresome to Women of your Nicety, and as nauseous to the Mind, as Meat often drest to the Stomach: for to be always in the high Road of making Love, a Man must Bake, Boil, Roast, Hash, and Mince his Love, to find Variety for his Mistress, who perhaps does not think, because 'tis brought warm to her, it has so often been cool'd by another, and only tost up again for her Palate. These common Practices of Love ought to be below a Woman of your Sense, whose Delicacy shou'd relish a Plate (tho' no bigger than a Saucer) of something new, above those vast Dishes of repeated Cramb. I am now in haste, being just going to wait upon the King; yet you see I prefer Love to all, and stay to write this long Letter, when it might be easie for me to tear what I have done, then tell you wittily, this Letter is an Emblem of my Heart rent and torn for you --- Meer trifling, and ought no more to pass for Love than Childrens Toys

for

for Riches, or a gilded lump of base Metal for true Sterling. There's something in true Love distinguishable from affected Passions, something of Excellence which can't be discern'd but by a Trial that the Counterfeit can't undergo, an intrinsick Value that has something more than Gilding or Varnish to set it off; and such is mine for you. Tho' we must lament the Misfortune of being parted, *My Dear*, yet remember we are to meet again with the greater Pleasure. The Tears, 'tis true, were on your side only; but believe me, I had my share of Trouble too: and give me leave to tell my dear *Clarinda*, that she chides without reason; for if she consider'd, she would find it impossible that a Man in Publick Business, as I am, can exempt my self from Company always. For my part, I drag my self from one place to another, and meet with frequent Occasions of being uneasie, but then the Thoughts of you, *My Dear*, and of your Love, relieves my weary Mind;

for

for sure I may endure a troublesome World as long as I am happy in you, who to me is the best Delight of it. Nature made such dear, soft, engaging Creatures as you to reconcile that part of Mankind that can deserve you by loving you to the Disquiet of the World; it would scarce be worth our while to live else. Yesterday I paid a Visit to my Lady ---- out of respect to you *My Dear*, and for the sake of an Opportunity to talk of her who employs all my Thoughts. She was very inquisitive what was become of you, and said a thousand kind things of you, and prest me very hard to know how to write to you; but I did not tell her, nor will, till I have a Commission from you to do so. From thence I took a Walk over the *Park*, where I ran over my Mind every thing that pleases me in you; your Fondness, that is irresistibly engaging, and appears undesign'd; your faithful Love, that I am convinc'd will never alter; the pretty things you say, and those you write, and

and those thousand Charms that possess every part of you; in short, *My Dear*, you are the Book I study now, and I will not quit you to range after any imaginary Pleasure or sordid Profit. I cannot tell why Love, which is the most Natural, as well as Noblest Passion, shou'd not fit our Minds for the best things: it enlarges the Soul, and I fancy my self better in several respects, as well as happier, since I knew you whom I love so dearly, so dearly, that even you can hardly love me so much; and nothing in my life ever pleas'd me so well as my loving you. *Redouble, redouble, Amour une peine si chere.* Adieu, my Love, I shall expect a Letter from you next Post; and pray believe that I am ---- Sure I am ---- Yours entirely.

Since I writ this I received both the Enclosed; which I send in hopes they may divert my solitary Dear. *Adieu.*

LETTER

LETTER V.

Lucina to *Corydon*.

My Lord,

IN spight of your Denials, I have a little airy *Dæmon* traces your Actions even into your very Cabinet: now this Familiar credibly informs me, you know how to send a Letter to my *Clarinda*. I'll take the Ghost's Word for a thousand Pound, therefore pray do not fail.

LETTER VI.

Lucina to *Clarinda.*

THou little Thief thou! firſt you ſteal the Heart we all coveted, but that I forgive you; then you ſteal your ſelf away; a Crime to Friendſhip I cannot pardon. They tell us you are in the *North*; the World believes it: but thoſe Diſguiſes are too thin for one who loves like me. I read in *Corydon*'s Triumphant Eyes a better Fate than your Abſence at that Diſtance in that cold Region; and rigid Relations wou'd be no Friends to the Deity he adores. Dear *Clarinda*, by our paſt Vows of everlaſting Friendſhip, let me hear from thee; for all the Court and World is inſipid to me ſince you have left it. Write to me, *My Dear*, becauſe I would not have the adorable *Clarinda* juſtly call'd ungrateful, which ſhe muſt be if ſhe forgets ſo faithful a Friend as *Lucina.*

LETTER VII.

Clarinda to *Corydon.*

YOur Pacquet came seasonably to wake me out of some melancholly Reflections which Conquer my Resolves against 'em, and too often seize my Soul, nay they begin to have an Effect upon my Body; nor will my Youth, and that strong Cordial *Love*, long preserve the Jewel *Health*; but your Letter has rous'd the darling Passion, and now I feel no Pain: Charming Pleasures shrill thro' my Veins, and Tides of Joy chear my beating Heart.

I am also pleased and surprized at my *Lucinda*'s Letters; and be assured, *My Lord*, your Visiting her infinitely obliges me; for if ever true Friendship possest the Hearts of Women, the Sacred Guest is lodged in ours.

Yet so nice my Notions are of Love, I denied my self any Joy but what

what you create: forbear conversing with that precious, peculiar, only valued Friend, left the little God should be offended, if I took one Thought from him: but her kind Reproach, and your Encouragement, have revived Friendship's Ardour toward that charming fair one. I have writ to her, and sent you the Copy, for I was ashamed (*My Souls Bliss*) to let it go thro' your hands, tho' 'tis to my dearest Friend. I shall grow bolder. I do remember well, when first I gave my *Corydon* leave to write, how I trembled at the wish'd Receipt: My Spirits fired my Face with Blushes, then sunk into pale Confusion; and tho' alone, long I feared to break the Seals. Now advanced in Courage I write to thee; I call thee Life and Soul, and all those fond Words I used to blush to read. I prithee do not give it so harsh a Name as Chiding, when I tell my Fears. The Merchant whose rich Vessel is at Sea, if all his Treasure's there, does he not dread a Storm? You are my only Treasure;

Tem-

Tempests or Allurements may ruin helpless me; the serene Face of Beauty, or the Frowns of Power, each wou'd destroy my Peace. ' Oh wou'd my Heroe quit the glorious Pomp and Dangers of the Court for my calm Harbour, for Solitude and me, how many various ways I'd find to charm! Sometimes, like the *Arcadian* Nymphs, I'd range the Groves and Plains, whilst flowry Chaplets crown'd my flowing Hair: sometimes! Oh Fool! this is Romantick all, as old *Prosper* sees the Day-dreams of a Maid in Love. You are fix'd in Glory's Circle. I sunk, never more, I fear, to rise; no matter, give to the Ambitious Honour, to Church-men Luxury and Power, to Misers Wealth, to fighting Kings War and Conquest, to poor *Clarinda* your eternal Love, and my Reward exceeds all theirs. You bid me write next Post; you see I do. Next, and every Post, I pray do you remember, and fear not, your

Clarinda.

LET

LETTER, VIII.

Clarinda to Lucina.

THE Lunatick, my dear *Lucina*, flies all Humane Converſation; and that is beſt; for Follies that are incurable ſhould not be expoſed: But you that take the pains to ſearch a wretch that owns her ſelf poſſeſt, what muſt you expect from her deſtracted thoughts? Reaſon I have baniſh'd, and then you'll gueſs what I am a Slave to. My Letters will be only filled with Ravings, ſtill hinting at the cauſe, the lovely cauſe, that will excuſe me, that muſt excuſe me to *Lucina*. She knows his Charms, has heard his Vows, and often whiſpered Pitty to my yielding Soul. Oh be kind to him and me! ſee him often, and ſometimes talk of her who always thinks of you, and whom you will ever find the trueſt of her Sex.

Love

Love and Friendſhip are the Idols of *Clarinda*'s Heart.

LETTER IX.

Corydon to *Clarinda*.

SUre Heaven has no pity for us that Love! If it had, we ſhould not have been parted thus long. I had flown to your Arms ere this, if the curſt Clog of buſineſs had not hinder'd. Let me beg of you to be contended for a little time, and you ſhall ſee I will contrive ſome way that we may be almoſt always together. Did you but know the impatience I am under when I am from you, it would as much convince you of my Love, as the pleaſure I take when I am with you, which is not to be counterfeited. Ask your own Heart, whether it does not think I am in earneſt in what I ſay to you; ſure it is ſo much my ſecret Friend, that it will tell you I love

love you. I will certainly be with you the beginning of next Week, and lye a Night where you pleafe to difpofe of me. I hope you have perfectly recover'd your Journey, which I call the *Pilgrimage of Love.* I am in torment for every pain my Dear feels. By thy Mouth, thy Hair, thy Eyes, and every other Charm, I conjure thee to take care of thy felf. Be eafie and contented, fecure of my Love, and of every thing that is in my Power. Oh, thou haft melted my Soul, and I fhall never forget thee. Could you be fo kind to quit all for me? Can you deny your felf all other Pleafures for thofe few that are in my Power to give? Can you forget the Splendor of a Court for me? I know you can do all this; and in return, I can only fay I love you. Next Week, nay the beginning of next VVeek, we fhall meet, my dear Life. Can there be a tranfport fancied greater, when I fhall prefs thofe Lips and wander over that world of Beauty. Since we parted how dully does time move on? But we muſt learn to bear abſence, tho' we can never make it eaſie to us. Separation will always be, as *Cowly* ſays of Life, an incurable Diſeaſe. How do you ſpend your time now, my Dear? Let me know how you generally divide the Day, that I may ſometimes have the pleaſure of thinking what you are doing, ſo apt are we to be miſtaken in our Judgment of our ſelves, we do not know the Force of our Paſſions till we have the experience of their ſtrength. I wiſh any Man could draw the Temper and Diſpoſitions of my Mind, as well as the Complection and Features of my Face, then you ſhould have a Picture of that, my Dear, wherein you ſhould ſee my love to you had taken a full poſſeſſion of my Heart, and that, that govern'd every other Paſſion. I have juſt now been reading over all your Letters to me, and I find it is a good way to move and encreaſe the love that lies in the Heart; and therefore, my Dear, I enjoin you to read over all mine, from the firſt

I ever writ to you to the laſt, and put 'em into the order of time they were writ in; and then, *My Dear*, run over in your mind all the moſt remarkable Paſſages that have happen'd ſince we knew one another: and whatſoever has ſhewn my Fondneſs to you moſt, think upon that moſt. Thus, *My Deareſt*, do I with you; thus I confirm my ſelf in that Paſſion which is already fixt in my Heart. You may believe me, *My Dear*, I have minded no Pleaſure ſince you left me, but thought perpetually of you; and ſo I wou'd have you do of me; and as a proof of my Love, I am deſirous you ſhou'd love me. Had I an Indifference for you, I ſhould not care whether you lov'd me or not: but I hope I ſhall never live to ſee that day. I ſhall mention your pretty Letter, *My Dear*, to *Lucinda*, with whom I am to ſup to Night. I go with greater Satisfaction ſince I have your Leave to viſit her; for believe me, *My Dear*, were it not for your ſake, I did not care if
there

there were not such a thing as a Female in the World, so indifferent I am grown for all the Sex but You; by Gad I am, believe me, love me, and I am happy. Adieu bewitching Charmer.

LETTER

LETTER X.

Clarinda to *Corydon.*

My Corydon,

NEver was I so frighted as when I read your last. I charge you by all our Loves, by all you hold most dear, by all that's Sacred, come not near us. What I wish'd at first I swoon at now: a remote Country for Silence and Obscurity! why 'tis the only Place for Tattle and Glaring Light: already they are alarm'd at me; my being clean, and perhaps a little different Mein from what they are us'd to, has set the Village in a murmuring Enquiry: Shou'd God-like you appear, the whole County wou'd be in Uproar. Forbear, *My Dear*, or let your Love think again, and contrive some better way.

Wou'd I cou'd believe you have read all my Letters over again, as I, were you near me, cou'd convince you I have all yours by heart. This, without opening my Cabinet, is the firſt.

Will ſhe then hear me! Oh God, what ſhall I ſay! I that have writ to Queens, now am dumb! Love chouks my Words, my Pen drops from my trembling hand! Sure this violent Paſſion brings Death or Diſtraction! Either gives me Eaſe, but you can give me Heaven, where were thy Beauties formed. I will not ſay more, becauſe indeed the reſt is Madneſs.

Then *Corydon*, how ſweet was the firſt inclining Glance! *Lucina* led me to a new made Grove, at our great Miſtreſſes Palace of ----- She walk'd on; I knew the dear Contrivance, nor conſented, nor reſiſted, ſuch is the doubtful Yielding of young Innocence to Love's alluring Charms. You came; what eager Bluſhes fill'd your Cheeks! what Fires darted from your wiſhing Eyes! your Sighs were many, but your Words were few; ſhort were the ſtol'n Minutes; the Impreſſion laſted ever, even for ever, on

Cla-

Clarinda's Heart. But then, *My Lord,* how long was your Petition? how long you whisper'd, *Do you not hate me?* nor wou'd you ever leave till you had heard with a true but faltering Tongue, *I love you.* You caught me in your Arms; where for that blest moment, where were our Souls? Sure mine was fled, and yours just trembling at your lips, hover'd on my Bosom. Oh *Corydon!* cease, cease to charm me; give my labouring Spirits Ease. Farewel. Contrive some other way to see me.

LETTER XI.

Corydon to *Clarinda.*

ANd is it possible *Clarinda* should deny her *Corydon,* the only Satisfaction of his Life! but you shall be obeyed in this and every thing: yet I must try how far your Love will carry you to meet my Wishes; for oh I grow impatient now to see the dear Object of my Soul, *Lucina,* whose desires in some measure run with mine as to the seeing you my Dear! But oh she cannot wish like me, because she cannot taste the Pleasures you can give! Every Kiss from you draws my Soul up to my Lips, then shoots it back with tickling Pleasures that runs through every Vein, so different are your Kisses from what I ever tasted. I kiss'd *Lucina,* who wants not Charms even to create fond Desire in the most rigid Breast, and yet 'twas tastless all to me. We have contriv'd

triv'd *Kenfington* for your Abode, where *Lucina* has promis'd to be your daily Visitor; and in her Company I know *Clarinda* won't miss her *Corydon*; forgive me, *Dearest*, I mean when Business calls him from her Arms, which I'll take care shall be as seldom as possible. Let wretched Souls who are not capable of this divine Passion, labour and groan under the burthen of State Affairs, I would only have *Clarinda* mine.

Let me know by the next Post, *My Dear*, if you approve of the Place propos'd, else I'm again unhappy; for it is impossible for me to live without you: think on that, and then save or kill your *Corydon*.

I also send *My Dear* another of *Lucina*'s Letters, to perswade her to what my Soul longs for, your Approach.

LETTER XII.

Lucina to *Clarinda.*

HAng me *(My Dear)* tho I am a Widow, if ever I heard so much of Love before as your *Corydon* fills my Ears with. 'Tis well I dote upon *Clarinda*'s Name: I hear it, I am sure, perpetually; *Corydon* has got a Custom to visit me every day, only to talk of *Clarinda.* I never was a Confidant till now: but my Love to you makes your Lover's Story pleasing.

Pray hasten to us; I am sure all things are in your power: and why you should let a Passion cool that may redound so much to your Advantage, is to me a Miracle.

I will tell you more when I see you: defer not, for what I have to say is worth your attention, and as true as my Affection to *Clarinda*, and my Zeal to serve her. *Adieu.*

Corydon

Corydon faith we meet next *Thursday*, which my pleafed Eyes fhall tell you whether I am fad or or no.

LETTER XIII.

Clarinda to *Lucina*.

THat which all the happy World wou'd rejoyce at, gives me Grief; for my Prophetick Soul forebodes fome future Ill, nor will allow me fuch a Friend and fuch a Lover: perhaps 'tis the effect of Solitude, and the Spleen, which your beloved fight may remove. Ufe no Argument to me relating towards Intereft: I have took an uncommon Romantick way to oblige fine Notions, that are remote from fublunary things: If thefe Ideas fail, I have no recourfe but to Death nor no Sanctuary but the Grave.

Chide

Chide me now, for this is sad melancholly stuff: the Company I love, nay I might say adore, may perhaps revive my wonted Gaiety: however, in all Humours and all Conditions I am wholly Yours.

LETTER XIV.

Clarinda to *Corydon.*

WHy will you tempt me again to that Place which of necessity must renew a thousand Reflections that will rob *Clarinda* of her Peace. I am grown almost into a perfect Stupidity: It is a kind of a dead Sea-calm, whose Emotions I am scarce sensible of. Your *Syrene*'s Voice calls me again amidst the Waves, the Rocks, and certain Storms. Methinks this second Desire is like your first, like the first Lure of Love which shook my even Temper, and gave me highest Pleasure and highest Pain. If I consult my Reason, how often do I wish for that soft state of dull Security, when all my Care was Dress and innocent Divertion? but comes Love, my Tyrant and your Friend, that whispers o'er our Joys, repeats your Vows, your Sighs, and all your Transports,

ports, I yield, I yield; my rising Heart owns your Victory, and urges me to fly where I may meet those charming Eyes.

Ask your Heart numberless Questions, if like mine it has been sincerely true, ne'er let any Idea in but mine, or any pleasing Thought but Love? This and much more I have to do. I come my *Corydon*, *Clarinda* comes.

I send to you my Letter to *Lucina*; I told you I shou'd quickly get that Assurance.

LET.

LETTER XV.

Corydon to *Clarinda.*

WIll being near your *Corydon* disturb *Clarinda*'s Quiet? What means my Love? Were I ill-natur'd and splenetick, I shou'd draw strange Conclusions from your Scruples, and cram my Letter as full of jealous Suspicions, as an old superannuated Lady of our Acquaintance does to her young Gallant: but I know thy Soul's above the common Wickedness of being false, and 'tis a glorious Virtue to be true, and such I know thou dost possess. Haste then, my *Clarinda*, and with thy Smiles chear the Heart of thy now almost expiring *Corydon*. I shall expect you on *Thursday* Night at *Lucinda*'s; I wou'd meet you at the Coach were I sure you wou'd not chide me; for thou art as timerous as a conscious Murderer, whose own Shadow frights him. Your
Friend

Friend is impatient for your coming, and my Opinion is, that we shall be less suspected here than you seem to apprehend.

Excuse Haste, and believe me to be entirely **Yours.**

LETTER XVI.

Clarinda to *Corydon.*

I Am come to *Kenfington*, but find neither *Corydon* nor *Lucina*: Forgive my Impatiency, which cannot live without feeing you. I have difpatch'd a Meffenger in your Search. I may excufe your Abfence, for my Hafte has made me here long before the appointed hour. You exprefs my Condition aright when you tell me I am full of Fears: indeed I am. Hope, Love, and Fear of a Cenforious World give me fevere Anxieties, but your Sight will drive all thefe Cares away. 'Tis *Corydon* alone can bring Peace and Joy to *Clarinda*.

LETTER XVII.

Corydon to *Clarinda.*

I Need not tell you, my dear, that I have not ſtir'd out to day, for that you may conclude by my not being at *Lucinda's* before you: You may be ſure 'tis no ſmall Indiſpoſition cou'd keep me within, when by going abroad I might purchaſe the greateſt pleaſure in the World, your company. For what Offence I know not, Heaven has inflicted this Puniſhment upon me, except it fears your Eyes ſhou'd rival it, and I became an idolater. Let me beg you to be eaſy and contented, as much, I mean, as it is poſſible for you to be, when I am from you I hope *Lucinda's* company will in ſome meaſure divert my abſence, and make the hours paſs more agreeable. To Morrow will come, my Love, and if I live to ſee it, I will ſee you, tho' my life ſhou'd pay the price; till then Adieu.

LETTER XV.

Clarinda to *Corydon.*

I Write, my Lord, by *Lucina's* command, to tell you how we have spent the Evening, truly in reading all your Letters. *Lucina* flatters my difease, and perfwades me you can never be unconftant, tho' I have almoft brought her to my Opinion: The firft Letters have moft Refpect and Tendernefs; the laft, more carelefs and familiar. Sure uniting, the Flame fhou'd increafe it, I'd give the world to know, whether my *Corydon* loves me better or worfe, fince I have own'd I love him. *Lucina* writes the next lines, as you fee by her hand.

Better now, but whether he will longer for your kindnefs profeft, I dare not fwear for him; I hope fo, tho' Mankind generally after the mighty
bufi-

bufinefs of a Conqueft is over grow Idle, and when they have reached the flying fair leave to perfue.

Hear ye that, my Lord, *Clarinda's* timourous nature creates a thoufand fuch apprehenfions, this dear Friend who over-looks me too too often fooths my fears, and fans my flames, by calling you excellent and Charming, Glory of your Sex and Age: Oh, my beft life, do you never meet with the pleafure of hearing me commended, I Court, I dote on your praife, but I am fond as artlefs, innocence as harmlefs Maids, who never were betrayed. Farewel; to morrow Dine with us if you can.

Lucina*s Poftcript.*

Oh, happy happy you, fure never Man was bleft like my Lord ------, *Clarinda* is a little World of Charms; her Looks, her Will, her Air gives me tranfports, tho' a Woman; what then,

then, muſt you feel; how can you forbear, the publick teſtimony of your love, and bind her ever to your heart, with that Charm which Death alone diſſolves; 'tis the only wonder I have in the Affair, that you defer.

LETTER XVIII.

Corydon to *Clarinda.*

JUſt as I receiv'd an Order to attend our great Maſter to *Windſor*, I got your Bilet-doux I know not whoſe properly to call it, for your Queries, Anſwers and Surmiſes are ſo prettily interwoven, that I know not who's the Miſtreſs, who's the Friend; that by the way, tho' *Corydon* is not authentick, for thy heart tells thee *Clarinda* claims the ſuperiority, tho' one wou'd ſwear *Lucina* were no ſtranger to my heart, ſhe knows ſo well its ſecret thoughts, and you may believe her, when ſhe tells you I ſhall be for ever conſtant, for ſhe ſpeaks my Sentiments exactly; and as to your Queſtion, whether I love you better now than before, I anſwer, better, better, a thouſand times, and the diſpute ſhall be hereafter who
lov'd

lov'd moſt. Now one word to your Friend, and then I've done, for my Coach waits, but all ſhall wait, till you're anſwer'd.

 Now, Madam, what ſhall I ſay to return your Civility, I can only wiſh I had another Heart to offer you, ſo nearly you reſemble her who has poſſeſſion of this, that I cou'd never make a better choice, and ſince our Loves are mutual, 'tis pitty there ſhou'd be any thing wanting to compleat our mutual happineſs, but impoſſibilities are not in the reach of Mortals; all that are allow'd to us, is but barely wiſhing, which does but inhance the pain. I have ten thouſand obligations to you; firſt for your kind thoughts of me; ſecondly, the care you take to divert *Clarinda,* whoſe pleaſure I wiſh equal to my own; and ſhe ſhall never find me wanting in ought that may conduce to it. And now Ladies both, I am ſorry I can't do my ſelf the Honour of Dining with you to day, but I know nothing ſhall
hinder

hinder the satisfaction to Morrow, which I propose in your charming Conversation; till when I am, dear *Clarinda*,

Your Faithful Lover, and

Lucina's humble Servant.

Corydon.

LETTER XIX.

Clarinda to *Corydon.*

NOthing but your dear Self cou'd be welcomer than your Epistle, which I muſt ſay we received ſince my *Lucina* ſhared it; but for my Life I can't get her to ſet her Fiſt to this: ſhe vows ſhe won't: ſhe write to a Man ----- no, ſhe ſcorns it. *My Lord*, Am not I mighty gay? Methinks I am. Ah this Sunſhine! 'twill not laſt, there is a gloomy Fate, I fear, belongs to me. My dear *Lucina* jogs my hand, and will not let me entertain a melancholly Thought. Hold ---- what am I talking on? wide of the matter: for you muſt know, *My Lord*, it is abſolutely neceſſary you Dine with us to day, becauſe there is ſome delicate, delicate, I won't tell you what: come and ſee. Make much of this Note, for I cannot tell where

where ever you'll have such another from ▓▓▓▓

See what a Blot she's made as I was saying Poor Clarinda.

LETTER XX.

Corydon to *Clarinda.*

THis comes to kiss my dear *Clarinda*'s Hand, and tell her I'm just wak'd from a very pleasing Dream: Methought I had got a Lady in my Arms, pretty, and witty, and kind as my Desires cou'd frame; I believe you guess the Person. Duce take Imagination, I say ---- for I ne'er had more mind to real Substance than at present. Now, *My Dear*, I must rise, wash my Mouth, and then drink your Healths in *Chocolet*; and I expect to be pledg'd by you two Ladies in *Ratifea.* Hark! methinks I hear that Lady dy (that wou'd not write to a Man) say, What does he take us for? I'll rattle him ---- Prithee *Clarinda* take up the Cudgels for me, and tell her she must either strictly observe the Rules of Quality, or resign her Pretensions to't; for that's a main Ingredient in the Composition. Hold --- I had like to have forgot Thanks for my Entertainment Yesterday, which was the best furnish'd Table I ever din'd at: Beauty enough to warm an Anchorite, Wit enough to confound a Statesman, and good Humour enough to baffle the Spleen of a Critick: these were the standing Dishes ---- The rest I remember were excellent in their kind ---- not forgetting the Venison which I think was as good as I ever eat. If possible, I'll see you as soon as the House breaks up --- but in the Evening I won't fail; till when, believe me

Your impatient *Corydon*.

LETTER XXI.

Corydon to *Lucina.*

WHat I left *Clarinda* to guess at, I must explain to you. The kind Lady I mention'd was your dear Self: wou'd to *Jove* it had been real. According to Opinion of the Learned, the Imagination represents the Image of things in the Mind, that are not present to the Sence; so your Image being perpetually in my Mind, no wonder that Sleep shou'd bring you to my Arms. Oh *Lucinda!* 'tis impossible for a Heart, tho ne'er so well fortified with Resolution, to hold out against Beauty irresistible like yours. Your Eyes disperse Darts of such magnetick Power, that you never fail to captivate whoe'er you look on. For my part, I own my self your Slave; your Wit has charm'd my Soul, your Beauty made a perfect Conquest o'er my Heart, and your

your good Humour has drawn my Inclinations into the Confederacy. I'm uneasie when from you, and not contented when with you, wanting opportunity to tell you how much I am, *Madam*, your passionate Adorer,

Corydon.

Shew this to your Friend if you dare.

LETTER XXII.

Clarinda to *Corydon.*

My Lord,

YOur not coming laſt night, occaſions this Epiſtle; it is ſent thus early to prevent ſuch naughty Morning Dreams, and ſuch bold *Billet Deux,* I aſſure you *Lucina* vows never to ſee your Face again: ſhe ſays you are a falſe, perfidious, barbarous ---- I cannot for my heart write all the hard Words ſhe thunders in my Ears: and this is all forſooth becauſe you ſuſpected we wou'd be ſuch a couple of Errant Lady Errants to pledge you in a Cup of *Ratefea.* Well, *Corydon,* if I make up this matter you muſt have a care how you offend a ſecond time: tho if I judge other Hearts by my own, your Preſence will make ample Satisfaction. But ſetting this Mirth aſide, which ſeldom belongs to me my Dear, thou
Life

Life of my Defires, Darling of my Days, and conſtant Image of my Nights, the perpetual Idea of my waking Thoughts, and Angel of my working Fancy when lockt in Slumbers, then even then, Beloved, I muſt leave thee again, Fate and Fame, my Enemies, thy ſuppliant Slaves, they decree that I muſt leave thee, read the encloſed and ſee if I can reſt in Peace.

LETTER XXIII.

To Mrs.---- *at* Kenſington.

Madam,

DO you imagine you can ſtay unobſerved near the Court, near your Relations, and in the midſt of an admiring World, who ſearch for you as *Perſians* wou'd after the Sun, were that obſcur'd; retire or elſe appear in Publick. Oh, be careful how you truſt my Lord of ----- and be aſſured it is a Friend that gives this Caution.

Alaſs, what Friend ſoe'er it is the Advice comes now too late, I have ventured all my ſtock of Love and Faith, ſhould you now prove falſe I have nothing left to looſe. Oh thou unneceſſary Friend, all aid is paſt like Pillows to the dying. I may be preſerved in Torture, but cannot live without him. Oh ſwear again, again begin the Tale of Love, or I ſhall fear

I know not what to fear; forgive me *Corydon* thefe wild Excurfions; *Lucina* knows not the latter part of this Letter, I wou'd not difturb her or you with my Concerns, for I am never, never fo happy as when I fee that faithful Friend and charming Lover pleafed, fomething I have more to tell you, which is not fo proper to be writ. *Adieu.*

LETTER XXIV.

Corydon to *Clarinda.*

IT is impossible to describe the concern thy Letter put me into, what damn'd officious Devil this unknown Friend can be, I can't guess for my Soul, but that it is some implement of Hell I'm certain, for none else cou'd be so bold to Caution *Clarinda* in ought against her *Corydon*, for if there ever were such a thing as true Love. I love thee, *My Dear*, what other proof can I give you than what I have already, think *Clarinda*, and if there be a thing in the power of *Corydon* to clear the scruples of the Woman I adore, ask boldly, and if I do it not may you hate me, which is the greatest Curse I can invoke on the head of your faithful *Corydon*.

I will wait on you inftantly to know the Secret, and tell you my felf how much I am

Yours.

I am fo intolerably out of humour, that I cannot find one Gallant Expreffion to your fair angry Friend, in faith you are both tormenting Baggages, and that I'le ftand by.

LETTER XXV.

Clarinda to *Corydon.*

LAft Night (my Lord) I well remember you made me promife to tell you this Morning, if my Mind and Refolutions were the fame: Oh! be affured I am not altered for all Reflections, but confirm my Opinion. I muft go that's certain, or be expofed to what will break my Heart, and why fhould you withftand it; you know I go yours, I live but to think on you, I rejoyce in nothing but my Love to you, which now is grown my vital part, and all my Health and Peace, and even Life depends upon my Paffion. You often bid me ask and have, and at the fame time you know I have no other wifh but you; do you propofe the Method for our Happinefs, fix it to your unerring Judgment, or be Love your Guide. I'le not fubmit alone,

lone, that is too poor a Word; no, I'le sacrifice all, all to make you easie. Generous *Corydon* can not use *Clarinda* ill.

The trusting, charmed, the loving, doting, dying, fond *Clarinda* come and help contrive my Journey, the time will quickly now run on in swift hours of Pleasure unobserved, if wants obscure will come, then the rugged Traveller will drag his pinnion'd Wings, and each slow beating Minutes march seems a long age of woe; but I anticipate my Sorrows; Joy of my Soul farewel.

Postscript.

Lucina is grown shy, and will not help me out my Letters, I fear wants sprightliness to please a Man of your Fire, my love is fierce as yours, that's all I boast of, *Adieu.*

LETTER

LETTER XXVI.

Corydon to *Clarinda.*

MUst I propose the Method to create and fulfil our Happiness? then let it be to love for ever, for sure there is no Bliss beyond it, for where two Hearts are bound by mutual Love, no petty Quarells dare intrude, or causeless Jealousies destroy their Quiet; Love and Honour are the only tyes upon our Actions, and he that breaks either of them will have no regard to Laws, we have had but too many Presidents lately, in *England* the Power of the Parliament suppasses that of the Church. Be assured, my Dearest, that I Love and I do no more know the time when I shall not do so, than when I shall dye. Believe me, and take care of your self, and me in you. If you are bent upon going, I will see you to Night, tho' if you might be

prevail'd

prevail'd upon to stay till *Tuesday*, I would beg to be excused till to Morrow Morning, since some Affairs of Consequence require my attendance upon his M----y in his Closet this Evening; but if *Clarinda* Commands all things shall be defer'd for her.

Postscript.

Answer *per* Bearer, that I may take my Methods according.

LETTER XXVII.

Corydon to *Lucina.*

WHat Conftruction does the fair *Lucinda* think I have put upon her concealing my Letter from *Clarinda*——— Why Faith——— That I am not indifferent to her---- Pardon my Vanity, but you can't in reafon deny me the liberty of making the beft Interpretation for my Love I can, fince to have a fhare in your efteem is the utmoft extent of my Defires, and the hopes of once acquiring it is the only comfort of my Life. Oh Madam, cou'd you but conceive the diforder of my Heart when I'm oblig'd to carefs one for whom I find my Flame declining, and at the fame time to entertain another which I know I'm Fated to adore, with cold complafance or artful Gallantry. I am almoft mad---- I have juft writ a fhort Letter to *Clarinda*,
which

which I suppose you'll see, for my part I have with the greatest violence imaginable forc'd my self to write kindly to her, Dissembling is not my Tallent, and 'tis with the greatest regret in the World that I'm oblig'd to practice it, and I am so much a lover of plain dealing, that I fear she'l quickly discover the Imposture.

I was under some Apprehensions that *Lucinda* was the Person that had caution'd *Clarinda*; but since I saw her my Suspitions are chang'd, and I look upon it as a happy Omen in driving her into the Country, to make room for my humble Addresses to the dear *Lucinda*, which in spight of her coldness *Corydon* will perform.

If you value the well being of a Person prefers you to all Considerations whatsoever, send one Line to your faithful Slave.

LET-

LETTER XXVIII.

Clarinda to *Corydon.*

THe three Words I sent by your Messenger, tells you I obey your desire in my stay till *Tuesday*; but having past an Evening without seeing you or *Lucina*, sure I cannot employ it so much to my Satisfaction as Scribling to you first, I wou'd ask you whether you think your self or *Lucina* happier than I, you make a Celebrated Figure, so does she; you give and receive Visits, have Circles, Levees, Ruells, she the same; I the perfect Devotee to Love and Solitude quit all this Grandeur, lost in Thought, feeding on Contemplation, catch but now and then a gleam of Bliss, and fondly think I am over-paid. Oh *Corydon*! why do you talk to me of Church or Parliaments. I study nought but Love, my Soul, that Heavenly Spark, formed

ed by enligntening Fire, but then in Bounds confined, and darkly fent in queft of Happinefs, centers all its Joys in you, nor mounts to the Celeftial Orb from whence the Infpiration came. Whoever is a perfect Lover can never be an Atheift ; oh ! they will find there's fomething more, much more, both in their Pains and Tranfports than a Mechanick Engine, plain Nature, like its fellow Brutes, cou'd feel; give them ye Powers but one Moment my wrack of thought, or my Delight, and they'l foon confefs the Immortal part. I fhall be punifhed for this I know, I fhall, but I'le go on tho' inevitable ruin waits me.

I humbly conceive you think me mad, I am fo, and I'le indulge it, I'le Love till I have forgot all other ufe of Life, ftill dote on my prize, my bleft, happy, lovely and beloved ; thus will I talk, and rave, and write, time fhall unheeded pafs, the labouring Spirits, when worn out with mighty

mighty Agitation, then will ceafe to work and all this violent Paffion be forgot. Am I not happy now I think I have been in the upper Region. Adieu, come and reclaim me from Romances, you have not ufually thefe flights from *Clarinda*.

LETTER XXIX.

Lucina to *Corydon*.

SUre fnch an Example of Falſhood no Age can Parallel, make love to me *Clarinda*'s Boſom Friend, write to me, well never be alone one Minute, it muſt be other Peoples Fates only can preſerve you, Houſes, Churches, nay, I beleive, the very Sky wou'd fall upon you if caught at convenient diſtance from Mankind; what vile Interpretation did you put upon my concealing your Perfidy from *Clarinda*; no, no naughty Man 'twas my fear to diſturb that Charming Friend, elſe I had thrown 'em at her Feet immediately, and ſtampt upon 'em; I beleive that you depend upon that Graceful Perſon, Mein and Gallantry to conquer all Hearts that run the dangerous riſque of converſing with you; bnt I will arm my ſelf with Friendſhip, Gratitude and
Juſtice,

Juſtice, theſe ſhall for ever againſt all your powerful Attacques preſerve

the incenſed *Lucina*.

LETTER XXX.

Corydon to *Clarinda*.

BEleive me *Clarinda*, buſineſs never ſat more heavy on my Soul than laſt Night, a thouſand times I wiſh'd my ſelf with you, if I am thus reſtleſs now you are near me, what ſhall I be when you are gone. I know not what's the matter with me, but I am grown uneaſie of late, methinks I'm never pleas'd but when I am in your Apartment at *Kenſington*; I grow weary of the fatigueing Affairs of State, and wou'd be glad of a retreat free from Court, and all its flattering Greatneſs, in
ſome

some lonely Cell with her I love. Oh *Clarinda*, pity me for I am now in need of pity; I cou'd curse every bar to my happiness, wou'd cursing do; but when I consider all things will have an end, I know there is no lasting Pleasure on this side the Grave, this thought arms me with resolution to endure the utmost frowns of Fortune, whilst you are well and happy *Corydon* can bear them all.

I'le see you in the Evening.

LETTER XXXI.

Corydon to *Lucina.*

YOur very Anger is so charming that I must offend again, to be again Chastis'd, I shall not endeavour to clear my self of ought you are pleas'd to lay to my charge, but plead guilty to each Particular, and throw my self upon the Mercy of my Judge, who can't in Conscience punish me, being in a great measure the occasion of my Crime; had you been less Charming, I had been more Constant to *Clarinda*; your putting me in mind of Judgments, I vow, makes me tremble least they should reach you, for Heaven never suffers Murderers to go unpunished, perhaps you smile at all the Mischiefs which your Eyes commit, and cry the Act is not yours; but let me tell the cruel Fair, pretended Ignorance will be no Plea in Loves Court of Judicature.

I can't help laughing at your religious fcruple; for my part I'm too good a Proteftant to think Heav will punifh us Mortals for perfuing its own Decrees; and fay you what you pleafe, I fhall never be brought to believe, ought but a divine Infpiration in my Love for you: Therefore, Madam, fpight of your Refolutions, I will hope, nor is it poffible you fhou'd lay any claim to Gratitude or Juftice, whilft you are deaf to the fute of your Admirer.

LETTER XXXIV.

Clarinda to *Corydon.*

Sure my Charming *Corydon* borrowed that melancholly Expreſſion from his thoughtful *Clarinda*, to meditate either on diſappointments, or the laſt period of our Ambition, Love and Care: The Grave ſuits not the gay, happy *Corydon*, whoſe Soul is ſo diſpoſed and adapted to his lovely form, that all his Actions move eaſy, and incline to an agreeable mirth and harmony, then his Manly reaſon frees him from all the little fears our Sex is ſubject to. I, moſt timorous of my Kind, am doubting ſtill, and frighting my Repoſe away.

Laſt Night, wearied with thought, parting indeed was the ſad Theam; ſleep came to my relief, but, oh, my Dream diſtracted me; methought my better Angel came, I ſaw the lovely Boy, his ſhining Looks confirmed him,

him, more than mortal, resplendent Glory filled the room, for my fancy worked me even where I realy was silent with Fear and Awe; after a tuneful sound I heard, I thought I heard distinctly these words in a Voice as soft as *Corydon*'s, *When first he whispered Love; ah, thou fond, foolish fair, whose Heart was made too soft for thy more rugged fate; awake from the bewitching Lethargy of Love, and lift thy Eyes to brighter glories.* At this he spread his silver Wings, and darting Beams of dazling Brightness, that my weak Eyes cou'd scarce persue the wondrous tract of Light; yet I did, and there beheld a glorious Troop in distant Air. I heard dissolving Melody, my Ears catch'd imperfectly the sound, yet the Words seem'd these: *He is false; and fair* Clarinda's *ours.* That Accent, tho' divine, waked me, with terrour I called aloud on thee, protested thou wert true, and contradicted all the amazing

ing Vision. Haft to me, my Love, and if thou canft not Swear new Oaths, run o'er all the old, that I may ne'er, tho' Angels fpeak it, believe that *Corydon* can be falfe to his *Clarinda.*

LETTER

LETTER XXXV.

Corydon to *Lucina*.

I Can no more help writing to the fair *Lucina*, than she can making Conquests where'er she comes. You are mistaken if you think your silence will make me desist--No-, I'm resolv'd to proceed let what will attend. Fortune still favours the Bold, and only Cowards fly their ground; whose Souls are incapable of glorious Actions, I cannot fear, having Love and Honour for my guard; Love bids me hope, and Honour pleads my Cause; and *Lucina* must be more than cruel to refuse 'em both. Tell me no more of your friendship to *Clarinda*, least I turn your own Argument upon you; for do you think she'd kiss the hand, that kills the Man she loves? To show your friendship to her, be kind and pitty me; I will not leave to persecute you, till in pure compassion to your self you condescend to hear me.

It was not without the greatest violence to my inclination, that I heard the tender sighs, saw the melting Tears, you paid *Clarinda* at parting, I grew Jealous of every look, and tho' she is Woman I envied her the blessing; nay, now, the very Idea of it distracts me; write, Madam, or my passion will hurry me to your Apartment; nay more, perhaps force me to declare my Flame, tho' a thousand Eyes were by. I wait the return of my Servant with your Answer, which will make happy, or miserable, Madam,

Your Ladyship's devoted Slave,

Corydon

LETTER XXXVI.

Lucina to *Corydon.*

ARE the moſt excellent of Mankind ſtill the falſeſt, when Nature gives every other Grace? Does ſhe purpoſely omit Truth and Conſtancy? Can *Corydon* forget his *Clarinda*, the ſofteſt Maid, the Gentleſt Kindeſt Fair, that ever yet was formed? Is ſhe not Young, Beautiful and Good as Angels are? Can ye forget her Love, her Faith, her Tenderneſs; with what a ſoft regard ſhe viewed her *Corydon* at parting; her lovely Eyes ſeem'd to ask it he wou'd ſtill be True, but he is Falſe, Forſworn: Oh, who ſhall whiſper the ſad Tale to her; may no officious Tongue ever reveal the perjured Story: Methinks I am guilty too, and conſcious of yours, I dare not write to my *Clarinda*. I charge ye, *Corydon*, return to your firſt Vows, and this one erring ſtep, this juſt growing falſhood ſhall be as ſecret

cret as the flames in Urns, whose sickly fires are never seen by mortal Eyes; but if you persist, what can ye hope, inevitable ruine follows; ruine on poor *Clarinda*, your self and me.

LET-

LETTER XXXVII.

Clarinda to *Corydon.*

WHat! a Post gone, and no news from *Corydon*: Is he not well? Or is he careless grown? Either is a tormenting thought; thou Blessing of my days do not forget me. Crown my solitude with thy dear Letters, and I am Content. Is that so much? Yet that is all I ask; I know my Love has business attending that great Monarch, who always smiles upon him. I know it is a world of care: Thus do I frame Excuses for thee. Oh, I must for my own Quiets sake, for shou'd I once believe neglect the cause my grief wou'd know no bounds, I soon shou'd grow the Image of despair, my wan Cheeks and languid Eyes wou'd fright the fools that are so eager now to gaze; away disponding fears my Love is Constant, his Vows are true,

his

his paffion all unchanged fincerity; methinks, fomthing crys hold *Clarinda*, he's a Man, and Men are all by Nature falfe, let 'em be fo my *Corydon*, not made of the courfe ftuff, the reft were formed, he is Angelical and all Divine, write to me then, and chafe my Melancholly Dreams, to guilty Bofomes, let not mine be the Manfion, for Love, even the God of Love, be filled with what Love flys difpair, tell my *Lucina*, fhe's unkind, tell her I love her next my *Corydon* adieu.

LET-

LETTER XXXVIII.

Corydon to *Lucina*.

CEafe cruel Fair thus to torment me, why do you call to my remembrance the only things I wou'd forget, yet this pleads for me, I never wronged *Clarinda*, and now repent I ever lov'd her. She is indeed all you can fay, nay fhe has Charms might fix Inconftancy it felf, but yours furmount, Heaven knows I have ftrove againft this growing flame, arm'd my felf with refolution to fupprefs it; but the more I endeavour'd to ftifle it, the more fierce it burn'd; fo that concluding the hand of Providence was in't, I ventur'd to declare my Paffion. Oh! *Lucina*, be merciful, as you are fair, and deftroy not my hopes with fuch fevere Reflections. Suffer me to appear before you, which I dare not do without your leave, fo abfolute is your Command over your difpairing Slave.

LETTER XXXIX.

Corydon to *Clarinda*.

YOurs I receiv'd my Dear, and can just tell you I am well, but so hurried up and down, that I cou'd scarce find time to write this short Letter: You must not be uneasy, my Dear, at missing of a Post, two, or three, opportunities does not always offer, and a Man wou'd not forfeit his Reputation upon so trivial a Concern as that of a Letter: I will allow you to write every Post who have nothing else to do; but for me who you are sensible have a Thousand things to employ my thoughts, you must forgive unlucky Business; once a Week, at least, you shall not fail; if I have leisure, oftener: For you may be assured I shall miss no Opportunity, since my time's not spent any where so much to my satisfaction as when writing to *Clarinda*, whose very humble Servant I am.

POSTSCRIPT.

I have not seen *Lucina,* nor don't know when I shall; you had best write to her your self, perhaps she stands upon Punctilioe's, and 'tis your Duty to write first.

LETTER XL.

Clarinda to *Corydon.*

SUch comfort as some sad Mother felt, when her only Son, the darling Heir of Kingdoms died, (can I add a greater simile) such Comfort did your Letter bring. Is it a trifling concern to preserve my Life, for of that consequence your Letters are. What will become of me? Oh, I am sinking down apace, my Melancholly fancy form'd this sad Idea long ago. 'Tis not my Fortune sinks me, but 'tis you, I scarce believ'd what I read, but thought my Eyes mistaken: They, alas, convinc'd me those well known Characters are yours. Be silent rather then write so to me; my Soul is great as thine, nor is my Birth inferior: Think not I have nothing else to do, for if you have left me I have great Affairs both with Heaven and Earth.

First

First I have a cause to plead with Heaven, my Youth, my Innocence, which the just Powers will sure forgive, and save than a noble Family; they'l not deny me refuge.

What pettish anger does my folly raise, I have no refuge but in thee, because I will have none, but do not use me so, least you repent too late, and never find in all your search of Love, such another doting Fool as your *Clarinda*.

LETTER XLI.

Clarinda to Lucina

Happy *Lucina*, if thou knoweft not Love, fhou'd I fend thee a Copy of *Corydon's* laft Epiftle, fure thy Friendfhip wou'd join with me to Curfe Mankind: But why do I complain of him, I am by all abandoned, *Lucina* has loft the remembrance of the Wretch that lov'd her. Oh, ill repaid in Love and Friendfhip, what I have now to wifh is, that you may meet a happier fate, a Swain, if poffible, more lovely, and truer far than *Corydon*: But as I faid to him, fo will I repeat to you, you cannot find a Friend more faithful than *Clarinda*.

LETTER XLII.

Lucina to *Corydon*.

I Have found your ill natur'd purpose by my dear *Clarinda*'s Letter; how dare you be so unkind to her, and have the Confidence to believe I shall entertain one good Thought of you. I give you leave to come and see me, only that we may talk of her, that I may convince you, never any Woman loved you more than she does, or deserved you better. Had it been my fate to have look'd upon you without injuring my Friend, I shou'd have thought you the most amiable of Mankind; but that consideration renders you the most detest'd. I am angry at the perverseness of our fate which scarce allows me to say civily, *Adieu.*
POSTSCRIPT.
I write to her this Post, I assure you, but what to say Heaven knows.

LETTER XLIII.

Lucina to *Clarinda.*

Stupified with Sorrow for the loss of your dear Society, I thought I shou'd never have brought my self into the Power of exercising any faculty. I am sure, now I endeavour, I shall infinitely fall short of expressing my ardent Affection to my charming *Clarinda*: If the Men are false, their own perfidiousness be their Punishment. Let us Love on. I have oftentimes a mind to come down to you, for there are things which I cannot, at this distance, tell you, that troubles extreamly your everlasting Friend *Lucina.*

LETTER XLIV.

Lucina to *Corydon.*

My Lord,

Last Night being vexed at your Addresses, and fond of my Friend, I have sent her something by this Post I fear will too much disturb her. Pray do you write a kind Note, to remove her suspicions and fears: Do this as you wou'd oblige one you profess more too than she wishes, unless circumstances were otherwise. You know who I mean, Farewel, learn to be constant, and then besure you shall be esteemed by *Lucina*.

LETTER XLV.

Corydon to *Clarinda.*

Had *Clarinda* been in *London* I shou'd have sworn she was just come from seeing the Fall of *Alexander* when she writ this Letter; 'tis so larded with Romantick flights, Prethee call back thy Reason whilst in sight, least it out slip thy reachs. Your Fears are all as false as they are unreasonable. What if the hurry of Business won't permit me to write every Post, must it then follow of necessity, that you have lost me? Indeed *Clarinda* you displease me with your Fears, and if you shou'd find what you seem so often to suspect, blame your self for it; for as nothing engages a Man of Honour so much as a generous Confidence, so nothing nettles him more than a perpetual distrust; why shou'd you anticipate your Grief, stay till you find me false,

false, as a witness of your Love be easie and contented, which is the only way to secure your *Corydon*.

LETTER XLVI.

Corydon to *Lucina*

I Am sorry I can't obey the charming *Clarinda* in every thing, I'm sure 'tis my desire to do so, but when she commands things so unreasonable I must disobey her, as I would the Gods themselves, (as *Lisimachus* says) Ah Madam! why wou'd you make a Villain of me? Why shou'd I counterfeit a Passion where I have none, no tender one I mean, doubtless I have a friendship for *Clarinda*, and shall have to my Lives end, but the better part of me is wholly devoted to the Divine *Lucina*; why wou'd you disturb your Friend, whose Repose you seem so much concern'd for, if you have said ought that may
disquiet

disquiet her in your last Letter, 'tis fit you contradict it by an other, but that as you please, for my part my Conscience will be clear; 'tis honourable Love I make to you, and Marriages were made in Heaven you know. Thus far I'm sure I'm in the right; now wou'd any reasonable Man think me mad, that after having obtain'd leave to wait on my Mistress, I shou'd stay to write to her? True, but what has Reason to do with Love? Nothing at all, --- and yet it has too, for I have a great deal of reason in writing this Letter, by which I hope to prevent a Thousand Interogotaries about *Clarinda*, which I protest neither to hear nor answer one, but every syllable you mention of her shall entitle me to a kiss; therefore Madam, proceed as you please with

your devoted *Corydon*.

LETTER XLVII.

Clarinda to *Corydon.*

I Will no more trouble you with my Fears, I alone was born to suffer, and so will with such a Resignation bear my woes, till I shame my severer Destiny, and make the World against its Nature, Laws, and settled Practice own I have been very hardly used.

Oh why did not this Almighty business press thus hard upon your Heart in the first persuit of Love, let an Impartial Judge consider, and in appearance you then had more than now, your Fortunes and your Honours were but growing ripe, your great Master had no other Favourite, the first is sure fulfilled, Ambition is satisfied, and the desire of Wealth is gorged, the King can live some hours without you too, all are pleased, only Love and I complain; where are now the soft Expressions, the bewitching

witching Language that ingaged my unwary Heart, then I was your little Cherub, the Angel Heaven had sent to blefs your days, and give a tafte of Joys Immortal; this and a Thoufand Words more-tender filled your Letters in the gay blooming hour of Love, when the leaft fcrip from me, wou'd fet your Pen a flowing, till Sheets were covered with exceffive Paffion. Now, oh fad reverfe, I may unheeded blot long Pages with my Truth, my Vows, and unregarded Love.

Of what ufe is my undoing? to warn my Sex fignifies no more than all dire Examples do that went before. I knew in Hiftory, in Poems, in many a melancholly tale of Truth how falfe Men were, yet I believed, trufted, doted, and am I fear undone, nay, even you perhaps may charm fome eafie Fair, tho' fhe fhou'd know our Story, for Women too often think they may fecure that Lover on which fome fad forfaken Nymph exclaims.

My

My Woman (when I will hear her) daily tells me how she meets with nothing but Praises of my Beauty, what desires I'd but vouchsafe to bless their Eyes sometimes, then I fly to my Glass, ask that if I am still so fair and young to catch all Gazers, why *Corydon*'s Flame rebates nor Courts nor Dyes as he was wont for his *Clarinda*. Oh, there is a mighty reason, tho' a most ungrateful one, I am his already and careless of the Conquest which with toil he won, his Heart grows fond of new persuits. I said I wou'd no more disturb you with my Fears, but 'tis impossible, they are inseperable to one who loves like me, forgive and love me if you can, if not remember poor *Clarinda* dyes.

LETTER XLVIII.

Clarinda to *Lucina.*

SInce I had yours, which I confess alarmed me, tho'. if I may venture to charge what my Soul loves, *Lucina,* with a Crime, I think she writes too darkly for that dear Friend I took her for, for if you know my *Corydon* false tell me the Particulars, 'twill be Charity to let me dye apace, such a wretch should not linger long in pains, in pains excessive, so mine I'm sure will prove; but as I said before; since I received yours I had another from *Corydon,* much of the same stamp, a little soften'd, but oh too haughty for my soft Temper. Ah my *Lucina!* I perceive he that was my Slave in the first Reign of Love, is grown my Lord and Tyrant now; well let my Ruin caution thee, believe not Man, not for his Oaths, his Tears, his Prayers dejected

jected dying Eyes, nor all the trains he lays to intrap our weaker Sex, either with me renounce 'em all, or Marry for Interest only, where Love is hardly ever named, but only Joyntures Settlements, and all the bartering Trade the prudent Practice; then you will never talk and rave like me, count like me the Midnight hours, and wake and watch till Morning; but why do I pretend to give Advice, who want my self Council and Comfort, Farewel. Write to me if you love me, if you do not let me be at once forsaken of all the World I value, and I'le soon forsake the rest. Adieu my Dear, my only Comfort.

LETTER XLIX.

Lucina to *Corydon*.

My Lord,

I Think I cannot better anſwer laſt Nights preſſing Converſation, than by ſending dear *Clarinda*'s Letter, which is juſt now in my Hand. I cou'd not read it without wet Eyes, if you can, ſure I with her may call you *Barberous*; Can you after this deſert ſuch Goodneſs, and after that think I'll receive your Apoſtate Vows? Well, if you can you are a bold Man, the Sin lies at your Door, I hope to have no hand in it: I think Repentance your only way to Happineſs; if you are obſtinate I ſhall pray for Grace to continue ſo as well as you, I know you are a Traytor, a falſe Ingrate to Love and *Clarinda*; therefore you ſhou'd expect nothing but hate from

Lucina.

LETTER L.

Corydon to *Clarinda.*

'TIs much past the power of frail Humanity to judge of Futurity, Madam, cou'd we set a bound to our Passions, and limit their Motions by certainty, we might set a rule to our Lives, and so prevent Providence which delights to show its Power by disappointing our firmest Intentions, I did and do resolve to love you, but cannot keep up to that effeminate fondness which I perceive you expect. I shall be always ready to serve you in the quality of a Friend, as much as ever, which Passion I think preferable to Love, I'm sure at least 'tis the most lasting of the two, and if you'l come to Town, I'le be one of your Visitors if you please to let me know your Days of Audience, and if you will promise to return the Obligation I should be very proud to receive you.

'Tis true Ambition is satisfy'd, the King is satisfy'd, all are satisfy'd but you, which shews that to satisfie *Clarinda* is beyond the Art of *Corydon*.

LETTER LI.

Corydon to *Lucina*.

WHat Man is there on Earth that has not sometime done what might pull immediate Vengance on him, were not Heaven more merciful than we deserve, we should all be *the Lord knows where*; but our Religion teaches us to hope for pardon of our Sins, and my sincerity for your Esteem; for faith, *Madam*, I am sincere with you, and when I cease to be so, may Heaven and you renounce me, a severer Curse even you, in favour of your Friend, cou'd not impose.

But why shou'd the fair *Lucina* hate me, because I can't love another? It is a very odd reason, and I believe the first of that kind that ever was given by your Sex. The Language of your Pen wou'd drive me to perfect Madness, did not that of your Eyes come in to my relief, they tell me a softer Story; nor is it possible so much Beauty, Vertue and Goodness, so nearly ally'd to Perfection, as *Lucina* is, shou'd want the forgiving Quality; no 'twou'd be the height of Impiety but to doubt it; therefore *Madam*, you see I am resolved to love you in spight of all that you can say or do to your

Corydon.

I design to wait on you in the Evening, and bring *Clarinda*'s Letter, with the Copy of my Answer, till when I am,

Madam, your most

obedient Servant.

LET-

LETTER LII.

Clarinda to Corydon.

TO tell you the sad Conflicts my poor Heart has undergone, if you are false 'twill but increase your sport; Good God, what have I done, what horrid Sin committed to merit such a Punishment as this? Why thou barbarous charming Man, why didst thou chose out me to ruin? Was I too happy? Had you so much of Hell to envy my Repose because my unspotted Fame stood fair, because I was adored and praised by all, therefore did you resolve to blast my Youth, and make me grow even hateful to my self: Oh most unheard of Cruelty, had I spread the subtle trains of Beauty, or design'd a Conquest, you yet had left to say, *She helps betray herself*; but oh your Soul your faithless Heart well knows I feared and fled before you; but you

I suppose laughed at my guard, and knew your Charms cou'd conquer every cautious Maid, they did I own it. I love you, dye for you; oh prepoſtorous Fate, can that produce your hate. You wou'd have me come to Town and you will viſit me, ſure you or I, or both are mad, can you behold me with indifference? Am *I* ſo altered? Are your Vows ſo ſoon forgot? No, no 'tis but a trial, yet do not, do not, cruel *Corydon*, do not proceed, 'tis too ſevere for one juſt enter'd into Sorrows, whoſe ſhining Morning promiſed a more happy Day; cou'dſt thou ſee me now thus in the ſilent Night, when all are lock'd in peaceful reſt, alone complaining and forſaken, ſure thou wou'dſt pitty me, ſure thou wou'dſt fly to my relief, revoke the cruel words thy guilty Letter brings, and healing my diſpair ſwear once again thou only art

Clarinda's.

LET-

LETTER LIII.

Lucina to *Corydon.*

I will not see you to Night I am resolved, I do confess I cannot help reading your Letters, tho' I am very angry with you, and with my Eyes too I assure you if they encourage you; one reason why I can't see you to Night is, because I am engag'd at my Lady ---- where I suppose you'd be welcome, as the Duce take ye you are every where, unless it be to

Lucina.

Postscript.

I have sent you inclosed my Letter to *Clarinda*; poor Thing, wou'd I cou'd perswade her to hate Mankind as I do, pray observe it when you read it, 'tis my real Sentiments upon Honour.

LETTER LIV.

Lucina to *Clarinda.*

My Dear,

BY all the Amorous Stars that Ruled your Birth, which I defie, I'll never love a Man, take your Advice, and Interest shall only be my Guide, if there's any thing so mad to venture, then at their own peril be it: Prithee do not talk of dying, live and make new Conquests, ask me not after *Corydon*, say only to thy self, *he is a Man*, and then conclude the rest; think on greater Miseries than the Disappointments of Love, and that will make what you suffer sit easie. I arm my self even for a breach of Friendship, because I have lately studied so much Philosophy as to find nothing in this mutable World is Permanent. I wish you happy *Clarinda,* I wish I never had been Born.

There now I think I am as Melancholy and as Sententious as you for the Heart of you.

Lucina

LETTER LV.

Corydon to *Clarinda.*

TO charge me with your Ruin, is to tax me with want of Gratitude, that I confess provokes me, I wou'd not have the least of the Creation think me guilty of a base Action, even to an Enemy, much less to one that I am bound by so many Obligations to be civil too, as I am to *Clarinda.* Faith Madam, you argue very well, and in the pritiest Stile imaginable, but you must give me leave to bid the Devil take me if I can or will believe a Woman of your Sense cou'd expect a certainty in Nature; Fortune and length of Days change

change all things you know, you may call me Barbarous, Cruel, or what you pleafe, but all Worldly Affairs are Tranfitory, as I am at prefent; for *I* am now awake, and muft go to Sleep, as foon as *I* have told you that *I* am more yours than you believe.

Paft 12 *a Clock.*
Corydon.

LETTER LVI.

Corydon to *Lucina.*

TO be Three hours in the company of the Miſtreſs of my Soul without having an opportunity of ſpeaking one word of what *I* ſuffer'd for her, was, *I* think, the height of Torment, to talk, and not to talk of Love; to whiſper, and yet not dare to whiſper the ſoft Tale, was more croſs to my purpoſe than the Game we play'd at, like *Tantalus I* had my Food in veiw, and periſh'd in the ſight of Plenty. *I* half ſuſpect you gave me the *Invitation* to my Lady ---- to exerciſe your Cruelty; *I* fancy *I* look'd like an Aſs, and *I* heartily wiſh no body diſcover'd it but your ſelf, for methinks a Lover when he makes his firſt Addreſſes is the ſillieſt Figure of the whole Creation, and *I* wou'd ſtill keep up the Name of Man, tho' Love rules all

my

my Faculties, and makes me act whate'er he pleafes. *I* read your Letter to *Clarinda*, and like your Politicks well enough, and if you can't be brought to my Terms, to exchange Heart for Heart, *I*'ll fubmit to yours; let *I*nterest be your Motive, whilft Love is mine; let me but reach the top of my Defires, *I* care not by what means *I* rife, fo far *I*'m a true States-man you fee Madam.

I defign to fup with you to Night, that is, if your Ladyfhip will give me leave; but *I* bar all Games, particularly Crofs Purpofes, nay even a third Perfon, fo *Tete a Tete* is the beft Company in the World, efpecially to one of my Conftitituon.

I am, Madam,

what you pleafe, by Heavens.

I humbly ask your Ladyſhips Pardon if *I* am too familiar, but *I* hope on our long and intimate *A*cquaintance *I* may preſume to baniſh that curſe of Converaſtion or writing Formality, eſpecially when a Man ſpeaks his Heart, as *I* am ſure *I* do to *Lucina.*

LET-

LETTER LVII.

Clarinda to *Corydon.*

My Lord,

I Am well convinced after the receipt of your laſt *I* ought never to write again, but *I* have already broke many rules *I* ſhou'd have obſerved ſtrictly, as my Sex, my Quality and Fortune required; your Inſinuations, your well acted Paſſion drew me into everlaſting Love, for ſo mine muſt be how ſhort ſoever your unconſtant date remains, and when Women Love then let them bid adieu to Happineſs if they love like me; *I* do confeſs in all my height of Glory, when the World call'd you mine, when at my Feet you ſwore the Prieſt if *I* ſo pleaſed ſhou'd make you ſo; *I* ſtill doubted, trembled, and by Prophetick Fears foreſaw this Fate, your Falſhood, yet give me leave to ſay

say *I* do believe since first your Perjur'd Kind, the first Innocence deceived no Story can ever equal mine, left in my very Bloom of Youth, one who loved to such excess, that in Romances only such a Character is found; one who made her God of you, and there's my fault; forgive me Heaven, like the sad Penitent *I* will return, and will never think of Folly more: But oh! how lame is that Contrition forc'd by thy baseness; Baseness, 'twas a hard Word, but 'tis a Truth, besides I deal with Heaven as you in the extremest fit of your Devotion dealt by me; I am by Halves sincere, and your returning kindness wou'd dash my Pious Vows; what shall I do? I am unfit to Live or Dye, to Love or Hate, sure my hurrying Senses will turn my Thoughts already wild to mere Confusion; relieve me Madness, relieve me Heaven, oh dearer than all, save me *Corydon*.

I said I wou'd no more pronounce or write that dear Name, ah spight of all my Indignation it hangs upon my Tongue and Pen. Oh, that as the Poets feign I might drink *Lethergy* here, and forget a few past Years; thou, guilty, thou canst Sleep, and scarce an Opiate Draught will lull my Sorrows; no matter, there may come a time when reflecting Horrors may break thy rest, as thou hast done the lost

Clarinda's.

LETTER

LETTER LVIII.

Clarinda to *Lucina.*

IS it then so ordain'd, that when *Corydon* is lost Fate has yet another blow and I must lose *Lucina* too? Had Providence in its severe Decree doomed such a Woe for her, to what kind Bosom cou'd I thought she wou'd have flown but to her *Clarinda*'s? For me there is no shelter now, my Family's incensed, my Lover false, my Friend as cold and as reserved, as all the Happy are to the Sad and Miserable. In this Retirement and Afflictions scarce to be indured by a Temper and Constitution soft as mine, I have found one faithful Creature, you recommended her to me, and sure Nature never made any thing so Compassionate! she weeps whene'er she perceives I do, tho' she knows not why, and her Service has no other fault but being too

impor-

importunate to serve me; you may well say I forget who I write to, when I entertain you thus, but my share of Comforts being very small, I dwell upon the shadow of one, a Faithful Servant, I fear I have nothing else to boast of now; I love you *Lucina*, but my Spleen is so great, methinks since *Corydon* despises me all the World shou'd, for after his proving ungrateful nothing will appear a Miracle to

Clarinda.

LETTER LIX.

Lucina to *Corydon.*

SHou'd I forbid your coming I suppose you wou'd not mind it, for you have got an assurance to take my very denials quite contrary; I have just received another Letter from *Clarinda*, and see the power of guilt, I dare not open it, but have laid it Sealed into my Cabinet; you need not fear I shall provide a Third if I have a mind to keep you to my self, had poor *Clarinda* been so Cautious you might have still been hers, there is nothing so dangerous or so likely to begin an Amour as a frequent Conversation, had not you gain'd good ground as a Friend, I shou'd never have listened to you in the capacity of a Lover; but whenever I wou'd entertain a kind thought of you, as, Heaven forgive me, I am too too often inclined towards,
the

the injured *Clarinda* comes cross my Amusements and damps all rising Joy, you have learnt long ago to appear powerful when present, nor can I chase you from me when absent; these are fatal Symtoms, and shew too evidently the approaching death of Friendship; but I will strugle a little longer, and deny my self the pleasure of saying truly I am

Your Lucina.

LETTER LX.

Corydon to *Lucina.*

Like a Reprieve to the Condemn'd, that's a Simile too poor, like—— what shall I compare it too, I, there's the Query, for 'tis impoffible to defcribe the mighty Tranfports which your Letter gave me; if the bare imagination gives fuch Blifs, what muft real Poffeffion be, too mighty to be born; oh my *Lucina*, for I muft call you fo, why will you ftrive to oppofe the Decrees of Heaven, for fure I am, that has ordain'd you mine? Why do you ftrugle with your Inclinations? Speak the kind Word, and fay you are wholly mine, do, my Faireft, blefs your *Corydon*, fay but that, and the Holy Man fhall joyn our Hands, and tye you ever to me; think not on *Clarinda*, but let Friendfhip ceafe till Love is fatisfy'd, and then

then renew your Vows; she cannot take it ill from you, if she does, let her expostulate with Heaven, since 'tis not in your power to prevent your Destiny; your Letter has open'd a passage to a Thousand Questions, which are too tedious to insert, since my impatience will not suffer me to wait your Answer, therefore as soon as I can be Drest expect me, for I shall fly to your dear Arms with a Bridegroom's hast, and tell you all my Love, and force that Confession from your Tongue which your Letter dares but half declare. Adieu thou Charmer of my Soul, for one six Minutes excuse

Your *Corydon*.

LETTER LXI.

Corydon to *Clarinda*.

I Have been studying these two hours, *Madam*, what I shou'd say to you, but your Sentiments of Love and Friendship are so different from mine, that 'tis no wonder we can't agree, I would have you act with Reason, and you'd have me Mad; thus while we drive different ways 'tis impossible we shou'd ever meet; I cannot for the Soul of me fathom your design, I still love you with as much Honour as ever I did, yet you complain; Is it possible that a sensible Woman shou'd prefer a Romantick Letter to downright Truths: I'm sure I shou'd like yours much beter were the Stile more Modern, nor shou'd I think you lov'd me one jot the less, indeed *Clarinda* you both disturb your self and me by your foolish Suppositions, prethee be more discreet, and think better of

Your Corydon.

LETTER LXII.

Corydon to *Lucina.*

THe dear remembrance of laſt Nights Converſation, and what I e'er this time to Morrow ſhall poſſeſs, have keep me as waking all Night as if I had had my fair *Lucina* in my Arms, I have counted each ſucceeding Hour with impatience, for every Moment ſeems a Year till you are entirely mine; I am juſt going to compleat what you deſired, and at Nine this Evening I'll wait on my Charming Bride; I have order'd my Chaplain to attend me there, who ſhall receive our Mutual Vows, and Crown my Happineſs with inexpreſſible Pleaſure. Oh! ſhould I deſcribe the mighty Tranſports which I felt when my *Lucina* ſpoke that dear obliging Word, *I will be yours,* it would

would require more time than I can spare, being impatient for the wish'd for hour, till which every thing will put me out of humour, all but the thoughts of my fair *Lucina*, whose I am sincerely.

LETTER LXIII.

To the Charming Mrs.-----

YEs, I will call you so still, and for ever; you are not less Fair because your Lover's Perfidious, the same busie Friend that cautioned you at *Kensington*, whom I suppose you laugh'd at for his pains, has taken a little more, and found you out at a remoter distance to send you such News as all the Town seems surprized at, Yesterday my Lord ----- was Married to ------. Now wou'd I be preaching again if I thought you'd mind me, advising you to despise this false Friend and treacherous Lord, whilst Beauty, Wit, Goodness, all the Vertues and the Graces are yours, rendering you too too amiable for the Peace of Mankind; whilst I say all this and more is undisputably your due, scorn the unthinking Wretch

Wretch who has ventur'd to wrong such Merrit; return thou soft lovely Charmer, return and glad the World and me, these are the wishes of a sincere Friend, tho I believe it will be very hard to perswade you there is in Nature such a thing, I know there is, and one that incessantly Petitions Heaven for your Happiness and Peace.

LETTER LXIV.

A Letter from Clarinda's Woman *to* Lucina.

Madam,

I Send your Ladyship with this a Letter my Lady received by the Post from an unknown Hand, the News it contains, whether falſe or true I cannot tell, but as it is I think it has kill'd her; ſhe has had ſeveral fainting fits, ſo long and ſo terrible, that we all thought her dead, in the ſad interval of Senſe and Life ſhe feels ſuch peircing Woe, that we know not whether to lament her moſt in the pain of her Grief, or Pangs of Death; I beſeech you Madam, either diſprove this fatal Story, or ſooth her Sorrows ſo to reconcile her unequal'd Torments; ſhe knows not of my writing, I humbly ask your Ladyſhips Pardon, and beg you wou'd ſend ſome Comfort to my diſtreſſed Lady. I am,

Madam, your moſt

obedient Servant.

LETTER LXV.

Mis ---- *to My Lord* ----

My Lord,

ALL fond Names for ever be forgot, and oh thou Charmer Love, that pleasing habitude of Mind, for ever and for ever be thou forgot, 'tis now ten Days since the sad Tidings came which publick Fame confirms, you cannot think what a swift progress I have made to that last Bed of Darkness, where even happy you must come blended in Death, the True, the False, the Faithful, Cruel, and the Kind, sooner or later all lye down and are in Dust forgotten; this is my *Epithalamium*, this my Bridal Song, yet I think I had not disturbed you with it, only I wou'd tell you how calm I am, how free from Anger, Fury or Revenge; Oh may thy Perjury escape unpunished both by Heaven and Men; yet let me warn my Sex, You fair Innocents, when like me in your soft Bloom, when Bright and Young, Arm, Arm your tender Bosoms against the Traytor the Destroyer Man; force your listening Ears from the bewitching Tale, for if you hear like me, you surely are undone; but above all fly secret Love, where headlong Passion leaves unconsulted Friends and Fame, where trusting your perfidious Conqueror, you think you are safe; such safety is in Storms without a Pilot, such safety in midst of Flames, in Pests, in Wars or Famine, such safety is the Honour of a Man whom Oaths, whom Love, and Thousand, Thousand Tyes have bound; with Flattery you begin your curst Artifices, what pains you take to raise the work of Ruin? Oh how I hate my Eyes 'cause you have praised them, 'cause they have been pleased with gazing at a thing so false; perhaps you cannot spare a blisful Minute to read this, I care not, I am not solicitous you shou'd, yet will I

go

go on, speak o'er my Wrongs, and fix in Characters indelible my Injuries, that being past, I'll write no more, no more complain, but lost in silent Contemplation disdain this lesser World, where Faith, Friendship, and all the Sacred Laws, both Humane and Divine, are broke; where Guilt and Greatness joyn, where nothing is sincere, nor nothing truly happy, and as my load of Misery exceeds whate'er my Sex had felt before, so shall my Patience, Resignation, and Forgiveness. I suppose you wonder I complain not of your Bride, I wou'd if possible forget that ever such a Woman was, as I will daily strive to banish from my Thoughts the Bridegroom; revel in everlasting Joys, study still new pleasures to employ your Sentes, for thinking will destroy your Happiness, especially if you remember me, which that you never may, I wish and bid you here eternally *Adieu.*

The End of these Letters.

A Letter to Mr. V---- *containing a short Defence of* Ariftotle, *in oppofition to a Modern Difcourfe on Comedy,* &c.

SIR,

I Wifh you may find the Task you impofe on me of any ufe to you, then I fhall have no reafon to complain of the Trouble; but I believe you are the only Man that ever read *Ariftotle*, that had the fhadow of a Reafon againft any thing he has faid in his *Poeticks*. You may reply, that the Author of the *Short Difcourfe*, who fo rigoroufly attaques him, muft without queftion have read him over, and if fo, that then you are not the only Perfon that diflikes him after reading. I muft beg yours and the Author's pardon too, if I am apt to believe that you have both forgot him, becaufe

cause you both meddle not with one Word that he says, excepting the Unity of Time, Place and Action, which if you remember *Aristotle*, is neither the only nor the chief part of his Book.

If I were inclin'd to Answer this Gentleman that is so severe upon this Philosopher, Critic, and Poet; I could easily demonstrate the unconclusiveness of his Arguments; but I shall content my self with a bare Vindication of *Aristotle*, and leave you and your Friend in the full enjoyment of your own peculiar Opinions.

And in deference to you, I will suppose that out of some Ancient Manuscrips unknown to the rest of the World, you have recover'd that Book of *Aristotle*'s that treated of Comedy, and which has been invisible above these 1500 Years to all the diligent Enquirers after it. If you have done this the Learned World will be extremely oblig'd to you, if you communicate it to them; and the *Square Caps*

Caps themselves freely fogive both your Pleasantrie upon them, and that for a Present your selves have so little an esteem for.

But if in reality you have not recover'd this Piece, really the misfortune is so much the greater, because all you have both said, is directed against a thing that is not in *Rerum Natura*, and you unmercifully treat *Aristotle* as a Scoundrel Delinquent, without a possibility of knowing his Guilt, or what he says to deserve your Anger: For the truth on't is, *Sir*, we know not one Word of the Matter; and *Aristotle* for all that appears to the contrary may be as innocent of what he's accus'd, of as the Author himself, for except two or three Chapters, all the *Poeticks* of *Aristotle* that remain, treat wholly of Tragedy, and that in so clear and demonstrative a manner, that 'tis beyond a possibility of confuting by Reason one Rule he advances. But as for Comedy and Epick Poesie, we have not so much left of it as can perswade us to imagine it defign'd as a Compliment either to *Alexander's* Favourite, *Homer*, or to *Ariftophanes*; for *Tragedy*, not the *Epopee*, was his Darling, fo ill a Court did a Man of Learning make to that great Prince.

Some Critics are of Opinion, that *Horace* took all that he fays of Comedy in his *Art of Poetry*, from this Book that is loft of *Ariftotle's*, granting that to me, 'twould not be impertinent to examine whether that which *Horace* advances on that Subject will not hold good, as well here in *Drury-Lane*, as at *Athens* and *Rome*, and then when we have done fo, I dare appeal to your felves, your own Judgments, whether it would or not. And if this be fo, why have you taken fuch pains to abufe a Man of your own Opinion.

I perceive by the Modern Author's Second Draught of a Play, he would have fome Order, Dependance, and *Decorum* in a Play, and that he does not think *Confufion* the greateft Excellence of Modern Comedy. If then
he

he had diflik'd that Model he fuppofes *Ariftotle* has given us, why has he not given us one more reafonable, and more adapted to the *Englifh* Stage? 'Tis true he owns that we may have a Play call'd a Hiftory of the World, from the Creation down to *Lewis* the XIV. and the Scene *Europe*, *Afia*, *Africa*, and *America*, with equal Probability, as 24 hours, and *Covent-Garden* and its purlieus; yet by his avowing his Practice to be contrary to Liberty, we may imagine he believes within himfelf, that a more Confcionable Compafs is more Eligible.

I fhall pafs over a Remark obvious enough in this Letter, that a great part is built by the Author on a fuppofition of *Ariftotle*'s being no Poet, which muft fall to the Ground, when in the Advertifement quoted from *Scaliger*, he tells us of an admirable Fragment of Poetry of that Philofopher's; nor will I infift on an other miftake of this Gentleman's, that all the other Philofophers had a touch at Poetry, dividing it into I don't know how

how many Parts, &c. when the Wit of them all amounted not to one of *Martial's Epigrams*; firſt he miſtakes, that all the Philoſophers had a touch at Poetry in the ſence he means it; for none but *Ariſtotle* have left us any Treatiſe of that Art; next I dare be poſitive there is more Wit to be collected out of the whole number of Philoſophers, than will make two of *Martial's Epigrams*, if not more; for I won't be ſo Dogmatical as this Gentleman.

But to obſerve all the miſtakes of this Letter, and rectifie them as ſome would do, would be to fill a much larger Volume than that which contains that Letter. I ſhall only aſſure him, that Regularity is not an Enemy to Variety, as the *Silent Woman*, the *Fox*, and the *Alchymiſt* of *Ben Johnſon* may teſtifie, and that the Irregular Authors have not been the ſupport of the Stage, as the *Orphan, All for Love, Venice Preſerv'd*, vainly pretend, and ſome others may prove. On the contrary the moſt regular Pieces of the other Poets pleaſe not. And

And now I shall only give you a taste of what *Horace* says of *Comedy*, and desire the Author to tell the World which of the Rules he has left us, is not of use for a Modern Comedy ev'n in *Drury-Lane*, and add only one Familiar Question to be Answered at the same time, Whether there be any difference betwixt *Comedy* and *Farce*, and what that difference is? Now to *Horace*.

Intererit multum Davus loquatur an Eros,
Maturùsne senex, an adhuc Florente Juventa
Fervidus; an Matrona potens, an sedula Nutrix
Mercatorne vagus, Cultorne virentis Agelli
Colchus, an Assyrius: Thebis nutritus, an Argis, &c.

Again,
Ætatis cujusq; notandi sunt tibi mores
Mobilibus que decor Naturis, dandus & annis, &c.

Respicere

Respicere exemplar vitæ morumq; jubebo Doctum imitatorem & veras hinc ducere voces.

To begin with the last, *Horace* advises a Learned Imitator or Poet to consult the Life, and thence draw what he has to say. Look you, there is the Gentleman's consulting the Poet, &c. *Aristotle* therefore is not so much too blame as he imagines if *Horace* has copy'd him, since he is exactly of our Modern Authors Opinion. He tells us before, that the Poet must make his Dramatick Persons speak according to their Quality, Age, and Nation; that a Shepherd, a Man of Quality, a *Frenchman*, and a *Bramin* of the *East Indies* should not talk all alike, without any distinction of Character. This our Magnify'd *Shakespear* has observ'd, one of his chief Excellencies being his distinction of Character, and I believe this Gentleman would not think it proper that *Dicke*, in the *Trip*, should speak like Sir *Harry Wild-Air*, &c. So thus far *Aristotle*'s

Aristotle's Rules of Comedy will fit *Drury-Lane,* and as for the Mechanic Rules of the Unity, tho' extremely conducive both to Pleasure and Excellence, yet they are the last dwelt upon by the Noble Critic in his *Poetiques,* which are full of Lessons as true and as excellent as these; and it is their evident Truth and Value that maintains their Esteem with all that ever read them, not the Prescription of 2000 Years. There is no *ipse dixit* made use of, and he appeals to Reason alone, and Nature in all that he says, and till this Gentleman can convince us, that *Reason* and *Nature* are things incompatible with the *English Drury-Lane Stage, Aristotle* will be admir'd, and of all too in *Drury-Lane* as much as at *Athens.* If his Philosophy had been built on so firm a Basis it had stood to this Day, and no body that knows any thing of the Reception and Rejecting of the Philosophical Writings of *Aristotle,* but knows there is no parallel in the case betwixt either his *Rhetoric* and *Poetiques,*

ques, and them. *Le Clerk* in his Logic, at the fame time that he confutes his Dialectics extols his Criticifm; but this is a Subject too Copious for a Letter, and I fhall keep my more extenfive Arguments till we meet: For to Anfwer all that has been faid againft him, a Man need only fhew what *Ariftotle* fays, as the Man that rofe up and walked before the Sophift that argu'd againft Motion. Before I conclude I muft fay two or three Words to fet the Gentleman right as to *Socrates* (one of the beft Men that ever liv'd without the benefit of the Chriftian Religion) he was none of the Sophifters, but a lover of Truth, and a confounder of thofe who built more on Form and Words, than Matter and Truth, and dy'd a Martyr for the Unity of the Godhead, and his Death compafs'd by *Ariftophanes*, in fome meafure, is now Honour to the Profeffion.

FINIS.

The Glorious Life and Actions of St. Whigg

Anonymous

Bibliographical note:
This facsimile has been made from a copy in the Beinecke Library of Yale University (British Tracts 1708 G53)

THE
Glorious Life and Actions
OF
St. WHIGG:

Wherein is Contain'd

An Account of his Country, Parentage, Birth, Kindred, Education, Marriage, Children, &c.

With the Lives of his Principal Friends and Enemies: Faithfully done from Original Writ, by a Fryar at *Geneva*, and Printed by a Jesuit at *Edinburgh*.

LONDON:
Printed in the Year, 1708.

THE CONTENTS.

Chap. I. *Of The Parentage, Country, Kindred, and Acquaintance of* St. Whigg.

Chap. II. *Of his* Aunt Impudence *and her Husband* Ignorance, *their three Children,* Pride, Rebellion *and* Disobedience.

Chap. III. *Of* Trimmer, Double, *and* State Policy, *their Pedigree, Education, Profession, Character, and Advancement.*

Chap. IV. *Of St.* Whigg, *his Virtues and Character; likewise of* Occasional Conformity's *Sickness, and of their great Enemy* Jure Divino.

Chap. V. *Of St.* Whigg's *Marriage with* Low-Church, *the* Bastard Daughter *of* Jure Divino, *with an Account of their Two Daughters,*

Schism

The CONTENTS.

Schism *and* Faction, *and the Troubles he had with them:* His *Separation from* Low-Church, *and Marriage with* Mitigation, *his own Neece.*

CHAP. VI. *Of the wonderful Change wrought in* State Policy, *and his Defection afterwards.*

CHAP. VII. *What became of* Pride, Rebellion *and* Disobedience; *with the Author's Digression.*

THE
Glorious Life and Actions
OF
St. Whigg, &c.

CHAP. I.

The Parentage, Country, Kindred, and Acquaintance of St. WHIGG.

ST. *Whigg*, however famous now in the World, was of an *Amphibuous* Production, and pass'd a long time for an *Hermophrodite*: His reputed Father was one *Hepperzelotes*; but St. *Lyola*, a *Roman* by Birth, really begot him, of a Strowling Lady call'd *Phanatica Porne*, born in the Suburbs of *Geneva:* From whence has sprung more *Saints* than from all the World beside, The Holy *Prophets* of old, and all the *Apostles* and *Martyrs* since, were but *Triflers* in *Piety*, compar'd with the Descendents of this *Sancti-*

fied Family of St. *Whigg*; whose *fame* and *glory* has almost out-worn those many *Worthies* renown'd in Ancient Story. He was a Man that was, in short, qualified for all *Imployments*, and never refus'd any, in *Church* or *State*, but was accounted a rare *Patriot*, and an excellent *Statesman:* Beside which, he was a fortunate and happy *General*, and what render'd him yet the more succesful and popular, was Alliance and Kindred with all the *Saints* of his his Time, which were more Numerous, than those contain'd in the *Primitive Calander*.

For beside his near Relations by the Mother's side, *Trimmer*, *Double*, and *State Policy*, and his three Cousin Germains by the Father's, *Pride*, *Rebellion* and *Disobedience*, His two Sisters in the *Flesh*, *Moderation* and *Occasional Conformity*, he had seven Elect Sisters in *Grace*, St. *Jonas*, St. *Lydia*, St. *Priscilla*, St. *Damaris*, St. *Tryphæna*. St. *Tryphosa*, and St. *Claudia* all of 'em his Country-women, and unquestionable *Saints*. Many great Persons besides, desired acquaintance with him; and some claim'd kindred of him; But *Plain Truth*, the *Sollicitor*, was a *Pestilent Adversary* to him, as one said, *Religionis Gratia, magis quam Mainte causa*, and spent all his *Oratory* and *Rhetorick*, but to no purpose, to make St. *Whigg* look black and odious in the Eye of the World.

The Place of his Birth is not certainly agreed on among the Learned, but in his Childhood he was Educated by his Father's Relations under his Aunt *Impudence*, and afterwards, when grown to Man's Estate, was sent over by by the Direction of that great Patron of his Order, the Famous Cardinal *Richlieu*, to perfect his Studies at *Edinburgh*, on the Northside *Tweed*, where he settled for a time, and grew such a proficient in the Black Art of *Schism* and *Rebellion*, that that narrow corner of the Globe was not able to contain him; so he made a step from thence to the Southside *Trent*, where finding the Land more *Fertile*, and the People more *Factious*, he at once settled a *Colony* and a *College*, for the Education of Youth in those Principles he had imbib'd in his *Travels* from *Switzerland*, to the *Ultima Thules*. It was in this College, St. *Oliver*, St. *Bradshaw*, St. *Ireton*, and all those Famous Disciples of St. *Whigg*, first erected their High Court of *In-Justice*, to Arraign and Condemn the 2d most Innocent Person that ever was, and their *Sacred Sovereign*.

St. *Whigg*'s Ancestors were *High flyers* of the first Rate, and they were the People that were such *Zealots* in the Council of *Trent*; where they unanimously Voted that grand Imposition of *Trasu*——*on* on the Consciences of their weak Brethren, and wou'd agree to no *Canons*, but what should thunder out *Anathema's* against every Body that were not of their Opinions; it being a Politick Stratagem of theirs, to break the Peace of the *Church*, from whence *Dissentions* might spring plentifully, and they hereafter have the Liberty to Build a glorious *Fabrick* of *Faction* out of its unhappy *Ruins*.

The

The Children of thefe *Righteous Forefathers* did not at all degenerate from their Parents; but as they had been *contentiously* brought up, fo they liv'd together like *Dogs* and *Cats*, not marrying at all, but begetting a fpurious Brood, full of *Ignorance* and *Impudence*, like their *Fore fathers*, each of them becoming the *Glory*, as they call'd it, of their refpective Profeffions: So this *Progeny* became the Joy and Glory of their *Progenitors:* But it happening after a certain time, that what they term'd *Perfecution* arofe on one hand, and *defolating Armies* over-running all on the other, they loving rather to fifh in muddy Waters, than venture into the clear ftreams where their baits wou'd certainly be difcover'd, chofe to dip their Hands in the Blood of their own Countrymen, rather than fuffer with a *Relation* of theirs which they difown'd, call'd *Extremity*, who Travelling into Forreign Countries, found out at laft a fafe and quiet habitation. But the Family of St. *Whigg*, quite otherwife inclin'd, was refolv'd to ftruggle for *Dominion* in an *Ifland* that was fo corrupted with *Divifions*, that the *Ruling Power* was always *obnoxious* to thofe that wanted the *Power* to *Rule*. Yet fome People will pretend to fay this *Ifland* is fettled in a *Temperate Zone*, an *Error* which our Times have corrected; for as it has not equal *Days* and *Nights*, fo in like manner the *People* here are never all of one *Mind*. And tho' there be no *Extremity* of *Weather*, as to *Heat* and *Cold*, there is *Extremity* in *Religion*, the People being

being all *Fire* or all *Ice*; yet they rejoyce in the happy Conſtitution of their Government which gives them *Liberty* of *Conſcience* to pull one another to pieces, for what neither of the contending Parties are perhaps poſſeſs'd of. Yet there is no *Place* where the *Deity* is oftner *named*, or ſeldomer *Worſhipped*; no *Place*, where the *Prince* is ſo much *ſpoke* of, and ſo little *Obey'd*; no *Place*, where *Peace* is ſo much *Preach'd*, and ſo little *Practis'd*; where *War* is leſs heard, yet *Diſſention* never ceaſes.

The *Agreeableneſs* of the *Clime* may be eaſily gueſs'd at, when we conſider the *ſituation* of it, it being ſeated juſt in the very *middle Degree* of *Moderate Latitude*, and in the very utmoſt and remoteſt Degree of *Roman Longitude*: Hither this Family came and ſeated themſelves, where they had Children, of whom we ſhall ſpeak hereafter.

The Parents of St. *Whigg* had but two Daughters, which were Twins, beſide this *Righteous Son*; The eldeſt was nam'd *Moderation*, the ſecond *Occaſional Conformity*: *Katherine de Medicis* and the Kirk of *Scotland*, ſtood Godmother to the firſt, and the Pope and the Devil Chriſtned the laſt in St. *S —* Chapel. They were *Twins* as I ſaid, and ſo alike, that you cou'd not know the one from the other. Both were Nurs'd by the ſame *Breaſt*; they were of like Feature, Stature and Diſpoſition, always bred up together, equally belov'd of their Parents, and which is rare to be found among *Siſters* in theſe days, there was no *Emulation* betwixt them, but an entire Love

and

and Agreement all their Lives; whatſoever pleas'd or diſpleas'd the one, did the ſame to the other; they both rejoic'd and lamented together, lik'd or diſlik'd equally, by a ſtrange and peculiar kind of ſimpathy of Nature and Affection. They liv'd both to be old Women, and buried their Husbands *Trimmer* and *Double*, who dy'd both together, unenvied and unpitied even by their own Family, ſo that they were deſtitute of a Burying Place; in ſo much that *Moderation* was forc'd to hang her Husband, in his Winding-ſheet, in a ſtrait Ally betwixt the *Church* and a *Meeting-Houſe*; and poor *Double* ſlept with his Anceſtors in the High Rode to

I had like to have forgot the grand diſpute that hapned at the Chriſtening of *Moderation* and *Occaſional Conformity*; The *Aunt Impudente* contended hard that the eldeſt ſhou'd be call'd after her; but the Mother oppos'd it with ſome warmth, whereupon the *Goſſips* took upon them to determine the matter. The Mother, *Phanatica Perne*, inſiſted on it, That if the Child liv'd ſhe deſign'd to Marry her to a Divine, fo that ſhe thought *Moderation* was a properer Name than that of her *Aunts*, to which the *Pope* and the *Kirk* agreed; for tho' they ſaid her Aunts great Intereſt might procure her many Friends, which were neceſſary to ſuch an intended Match, yet they ſaid on the other hand *Moderation*, wou'd have fewer Enemies; the ſame, or ſuch like Reaſons were urg'd for *Occaſional Conformity*, and ſo they took their chance in the World: But

it

it made no matter which was which, for not only their Age, Habit and Complexion were alike, but their Difpofition to, fo that it was a fmall miftake if you had call'd either of them *Moderation* or *Occafional Conformity*; for the one was as true a Friend to *Religion* as the other.

As I have faid before, St. *Whigg* was the only Son of his Parents, born when his Mother was well in years; he was Educated at a *School* which his *Unkle* and *Aunt* kept on purpofe to train up Youth, in the Principles of *Religion* and *Polity*, which St. *Lyola* left behind him as a Legacy to *Phanatica Porne*. This St. *Whigg* whas quick and apprehenfive to conceive and retain whatever he Heard or Read ; and befides, it was obferv'd in him, that he was always very inquifitive to dive into the *Polity* of the *National Religion*, which was wonder'd at in one of his Age efpecially : But what was more obfervable, he never troubled his head with *Confcientious Niceties*; fo that it was agreed on by all hands that he wou'd make a great *Statefman*, and be Eminent in the moft powerful Empires of the World, which accordingly fell out as the ftory will inform you.

B   CHAP.

CHAP. II.

Of his Aunt Impudence *and her Husband* Ignorance, *their three Children,* Pride, Rebellion *and* Disobedience; *their Characters and Imployment, and how* St. Whigg *was bred among them.*

Impudence being born of an Ancient Family, and having both a confiderable *Fortune* and Mighty Refpect among the *Quality*, made a very great *Figure* in the World; fo that it occafion'd *Ignorance*, who was a very great *Beau*, to make Court to her, and in a fhort time he Married her: Now *Ignorance* was a conceited *Fop*, fond of himfelf, and car'd for no Body elfe; he had a fine Eftate, and was newly come of Age, but a willful heady young Fellow he was, and wou'd neither be *Contradicted* nor *Advis'd*. He wou'd never regard or take Notice of his Wife *Impudence*, till he had fpent his *Patrimony*, and then fhe wrought a change in him. She had three Sons by him, call'd, *Pride*, *Rebellion* and *Difobedience*, all three too like the *Parents*.

Pride was a Beautiful fine Boy, but deadly ill natur'd, and delighted in nothing but *Gew-gaws* and *Ribbonds*, which he wou'd trifle away his time with till he grew to Mans Eftate. His Father fpoil'd him, by making a Pett of him, and breeding him up in all

manner

manner of *Pleasure* and *Delicacy*, to make a Gentleman of him, because he was the Eldest.

Rebellion the *Second Son*, being of a Turbulent Temper, was sent to a great Town to be put to a Trade; for he was a Robust Boy, but very dull at Learning, and hardly brought to settle to any thing, or stay with any Master. His cheif delight was in *Cudgells*, *Wrestling*, *Foot-ball-playing*, &c. by which means he herded much with the *Mob* at *Bull-baitings*, *Cockings*, and the like; and at last, grew so Troublesome and Tumultuous, that he wou'd raise the Neighbouring *Prentice Boys* to break his Masters Windows, and commit such Riots in the Street every Night, that the *Counter*, *Bridewell*, and the *Round-house*, were as familiar to him as his Victuals.

Disobedience the *Third Son*, if it is possible was worst of all; for he was a *Prodigal*, *Obstinate* Young Fellow, that wou'd do just what he pleas'd without Controul, and what was singular in his *Character*, all Perswasions made him resolutely bent to act the quite contrary, tho' what you perswade him to, was agreeable to his own Sentiments. From the time that he cou'd go alone he was out of the Command of his *Father* and *Mother*, on whom he was sure to exercise all his ill nature: His *Comrades* at the same time were capable of leading him where-ever they pleas'd, into all manner of *Follies* and *Debauchery*, which made

made him so Headstrong, he delighted in nothing but *Mischeif* and *Destruction*.

When these young Fellows came abroad into the World, and People beheld their Carriage, every body guess'd whose Children they were, and some imputed their faults to the Father, others to the Mother, but all agreed that *Three* such Children, cou'd never have been so Educated but under *two* such Parents; who both pretended to Instruct the rest of the World, but receive Instruction from none; however, *Ignorance* having now made away all his Estate, and his *Wifes Portion* too, was at last fain to Live upon his *Wifes Impudence*; and she maintain'd him and all his Children very *Grand*.

She taught a *School*, and was excellently qualified for that employment; a mighty Critick she was, and understood the *Classicks* to a nicety; *Æsop*, or *Apulenis* with his *Golden Ass*, was a Fool to her at *Reflections*, such a curious *observer* she was of what she read, or had occurred in her time, that she was universally vers'd in all *Histories* whatsoever, *Ecclesiastical* or *Civil*, *Ancient* or *Modern*; she carry'd a *Chronological* Table always in her *Head*, by which, she wou'd correct the most perfect in her time: All the remarkable Accidents and Occurrences that happen'd in her Life, she had at her Fingers ends, which you will say is rare Memory indeed.

She cou'd tell by variety of Examples, and plenty of Instances, what had made Princes

Happy

Happy or Unfortunate ; what wou'd make a Commonwealth Flourish or Decay ; what wou'd Raise or Ruin a Family ; what wou'd Settle or Disturb the *Churches Peace* ; in a word, you cou'd hardly put that to her which she cou'd not satisfy you in ; she cou'd tell you who or what was like to Thrive or Miscarry ; what *Match* was like to prove Well or Ill ; and her Judgment seldom fail'd her. She had an *Aphorism* which was frequently and familiarly in her Mouth, and call'd it an infallible *Maxim*, by which you might guess at what was *future* by what was past.

With her St. *Whigg* had much of his Breeding ; and he was careful to Treasure up his *Aunt Impudence*'s *Aphorisms*, as so many *Jewels* of *Gold:* Nay, in every matter of Moment he wou'd still come and advise with his *Aunt* to his dying day, for she long outliv'd St. *Whigg* ; who when he came from the *University* wou'd always visit her, and us'd to think his *Time* well spent: He wou'd often confess, that he had learn'd that from her Mouth, which he might have look'd for long enough in the *Libraries* of the Learned, and not have met withal in all the *Schools* of the *Philosophers*.

She had not, as 'twas thought by some, much of *Learning* or *Languages*, and knew none but her *Mother Tongue :* She wou'd quote all the Writings of the *Ancients* and the *Moderns*, of all *Faculties* and *Professions*, as if she had been perfect Mistress of 'em ; nay, her

Ipsa

Ipsa dixit pass'd for as plain *Demonstration* as any in *Euclid*; and *Aristotle's Authority* in the *Schools*, was nothing to hers in her *Private Closet*. St. *Whigg* was bred up in her *School* as I said, and profited much; was the most plyable *Schollar* she had, and therefore she took the more delight to discourse with him, and read him many a long *Lecture*. She wou'd sometimes take him in Private into her *Closet*, and say to him, *Dear* Whigg *thou art my near Kinsman, I love thy very Name; I wou'd there were more of it; and next to my Three Sons, I love thee better than any Relation I have, and above any other Mortal Creature whatsoever*; thy Name and Nature being so full of Popularity, because so full of Republican Principles, which brings us Mortals on Earth to the nearest Affinity with those Immortal Heroes who bravely defy'd Heaven and all its Power of old; well I protest shou'd I ever have another Son, I wou'd call him by thy Name.

I'll tell thee what dear *Nephew*, I have observ'd and know to be true, thy Ancestors have been the Plague of Mankind in all Ages, and in whatsoever Countries they have liv'd, have dishonour'd their Maker, Transplanted Peace, Rais'd Discord, Commotions, and Insurrections, Countenanc'd Deism and Impiety, Banish'd Loyalty, Invaded Innocency, Establish'd Schism, and Confirm'd all these where-ever they have erected Commonwealths; to enslave the lower World, with War, Contention, and Anarchy; and Curse the Earth with perpetual Enmity, Dissimulation, and Fraud.

Let

[15]

Let me advise thee my Child, continu'd the old Hag, *to hearken to the Aged in days ; if thou lovest thy Life and Prosperity, let thy Sister* Moderation *be known unto all Men.*

In the next place, in whatever state thou art imyloy'd, encourage that itching and bewitching evil call'd Novelty ; for I will assure thee she is of thy Kindred and thy Fathers House, therefore cherish all those that are given to Innovations and Change, for they are of thy own Blood : Set a mark on all those that cry out against Schism, that fruitful seed of our Family, and have no Commerce with those reconcilers of Divisions, who call themselves the Righteous Sons of Jure Divino, *for they are of a powerful and prevailing Spirit, therefore meddle not with them at all.* This and much more to the same purpose did Impudence *say to* St. Whigg, *and such like precepts she gave to all her Disciples.*

When *Pride, Rebellion,* and *Disobedience* came to visit her, she wou'd be Tutering them after this manner ; *You are Young my Sons, and I am Old ; I have seen many changes, and I hope you will see more ; I have seen War and Peace, and Peace and War, which I hope you will never see an end of ; I have liv'd Publickly and seen many Jolly days ; and you are hopeful young Men in these times, and fit for Publick Implyments ; therefore remember your Birth, and never shame your Parents : Drive on no Interest or Designs but those of your own ; Contend for nothing but what your Fore-fathers contended for, Impiety, Discord and Confusion ; Oppose and*

Detest

Detest nothing so much as Religion, Honesty, and Forgiveness; Rebel against all your Governours, hate your Country, and dispise the Church, then you will have your Mothers Prayers, and your Father's Blessing; you'll surely be prefer'd by your Prince, and valued by the People: Lastly, let me charge you in whatsoever place you are, to have regard to your near Relations St. Whigg, and never forget his two Sisters, Moderation and Occasional Conformity.

CHAP.

CHAP. III.

Of Trimmer, Double, *and* State Policy, *their* Pedegree, Education, Profeſſion, Character, *and* Advancement.

NOw leaving *Impudence* with her Three Sons, *Pride, Rebellion,* and *Diſobedience* together, I ſhall launch out into another Branch of St. *Whigg*'s Kindred, *viz. Trimmer, Double,* and *State Policy*; theſe came of an Ancient *Roman* Family, *Gallio* was their Grandfather, and *Portius Feſtus* their Father: While they were young, they were bred together under the ſame Tutors; towardly and hopeful Children all, being the forwardeſt Boys of their ſtanding, reading the ſame Authors, and performing the ſame Exerciſe, and profited ſo much, that in a ſhort time they were ſent to the *Univerſity*; where all Three were taken notice of for their extraordinary Acquirements and Diligence, their early riſing to Study, and their late ſitting up at the *Bottle*. There when they had taken their ſeveral *Degrees*, *Double* firſt remov'd from thence to the *Inns of Court*, where he grew a mighty *Beau*, out-topping all the young fluttring Fellows of the Town; The Reaſons and Grounds of the *Law* was none of his *Study*, but the Converſation of the *Beau Monde*: The piercing into the more

C knotty

knotty Intricacies and profound Mifteries of his Profeffion, was none of his Bufinefs ; but *Criticifm* and *Poetry* where the *Talents* for which he was fam'd among the Men of *Belle Lettres* : Notwithftanding this he was call'd to the Bar, and in fhort time became Famous for his *Practice :* He was a fine nice Gentleman, and efteem'd for his quick Apprehenfion, clear Head, firm Memory, free Expreffion, and excellent Oratory ; and what rendred him ftill the more Eminent, he was perfectly Impartial, not valuing the Client or the Caufe, but only regarded the *Fee*, and that not whofe it was, but what it was. He was in a little time afterwards advanc'd to the Higheft Poft of the *Law*, where he fhone like the *Moon* among the leffer *Stars* ; never Man was more extoll'd for a *Patriot*, and never none diffembled it better.

State Policy was the next that left the *University*, and he had a fancy to be a Courtier, being of the *Epicene Gender* ; he was a quiet peaceable Man, and conformable to any Government ; he never expreft much zeal or regard to *Religion* of any kind, nor was he ever known to go to *Prayers* by himfelf or look into the *Bible :* A piece of *Tacitus Livy* or *Machiavel*, he wou'd often difcourfe of, and feem'd to relifh, but talk'd very loofely of *Mofes* and the *Prophets* ; and for *Seneca*, in his judgment, he prefer'd before St. *Paul* and all the *Apoftles*, which he cenfur'd as well meaning Credulous Men, that might be eafily impos'd impos'd upon. Many thought him little better than an *Atheist* in his Heart, but his particular Friends knew him for a profeſt *Deiſt*. In times of *Peace*, he had a *Commiſſion* for the *Peace*, and was in Authority, and did ſingular ſervice in keeping his Country quiet, becaſe he wou'd never *Act*; and the Neighbours were forc'd to end the differences among themſelves as they began 'em, except now and then he wou'd put down ſome little *Alehouſe* where his *Footmen* us'd to *Tipple*. In time of *War* he had a *Command*, and us'd the ſame Diſcipline among his Soldiers as he did before among his *Neighbours*; as for *Plundering* and *Robbing* he wou'd puniſh them, but *Whoring* and *Swearing* he held for *Venial Sins*. When the War was ended, he had a conſiderable Place at *Court* given him, and *Moderation* being the moſt Faſhionable Lady there at that time, and in greateſt Favour; *State Policy* found, the only way to *puſh* his *Fortune* now, was to make pretenſions to her, which he did with very good Succeſs, and in a few days was Marry'd to her by the approbation and conſent of the whole Court: They liv'd together ſeveral years, and made a great Figure in the World.

State Policy had by *Moderation* many *Sons* and *Daughters*, his Sons were all bred with ſuch *Literature* as was fit for Gentlemen: The Eldeſt Travell'd to *Italy* to ſee the Ancient *Commonwealths* of *Venice*, and that little flouriſhing State of *Genoa*, and after his return

turn was bred a *Courtier*; and in a few years time obtain'd a *White Staff*. The Second was a *Soldier* bred in the *Low Countries*, who at his first return, his Mother *Moderation* made a Member of Parliament, and then got him a *Regent*. The Third was a *Physician*, who Travell'd through *Germany* and *Holland*, and took his *Degrees* at *Leyden*; His Name was *Temerarius*, who was so Famous among all St. *Whigg*'s *Kindred*, that he was soon made the Princes chief *Physician*, and no Body of *Quality* durst venture to depart this World without *Temerarius* his *Pass-port*. The Fourth Son call'd *Dolosus* was bred a *Merchant*, but at last, by the Instigation of his Three Relations, *Pride*, *Rebellion*, and *Disobedience*, and under the Protection of his Cousin St. *Whigg*, he turn'd a *Pyrate*, and afterwards brought great Riches home, which he distributed among his Friends, in order to procure him a free Pardon; which they failing to do, poor *Dolosus* swung among the common Herd of *Malefactors* who were Executed with him for the same *Crime*. The Youngest Son he made a *Schollar*, this was a Witty Pleasant Fellow, and had a Vein of Poetry, which he being too free with, met with the common Fate of the *Satyrists* of his time, and was severely lash'd for his *Liberty*: Notwithstanding his depending on St. *Whigg* and his Family, to be his *Advocates*, they left him in the lurch as they had done his Brother *Dolosus*; and so he spent the remainder of his Life in

a merry

a merry ſtarving Condition, having nothing left him to ſubſiſt on, but the produce of a *Ballad* or a *Lampoon* now and then to buy him a Dinner with; as for Cloaths, they were as Uſeleſs to him as Money to a *Miſer*.

Moderation had likewiſe by her ſaid Husband, *State Policy*, Four Daughters, the Two firſt call'd *Blandula* and *Crapula* were Ladies of Honour to the Queen: The Third call'd *Circe*, cou'd Sing and Dance rarely well, and was the Life of all the *Opera*'s in Town; ſhe talk'd *French* and *Italian* very perfect, and was abſolute Miſtreſs of all the Forreign *Romances*; but as for the *Old* and *New-Teſtament* ſhe never read a Page in her Life. *Spatuloſa* the Youngeſt, was the Talleſt and Handſomeſt Woman of 'em all; an abſolute Beauty, and ſo cunning in her Temper you never cou'd Anger her: She had a Graceful Mein that took with every Body, and had you ſeen her at *Church*, which was a rare thing, you wou'd think you had ſeen an *Angel*; ſhe was Serious or Pleaſant, *Hippiſte* or Facetious, Witty or Dull, juſt as her Company was.

They were all Four the very *Bells* of the *Court*; but to tell you how they ſpent their time, and what was their employment, wou'd have been a ſtrange ſtory to our Grand-mothers had they been alive again, and is ſtrange enough to ſome Ladies that live long after them: The Morning was all taken up at their *Toilets*, with *Dreſſing*, *Painting*, *Powdering* and *Patching*; the Afternoon uſually ſpent in *Visits* or a *Play-house*, and at *Night* a *Pack of Cards*: Thefe were the Books they were moſt read in, and had them more in their Hands than any other. They all frequented the *Play-houſe* more than the *Church*, and were more attentive there than here; Twice or Thrice a Month was fair to go to Church, but at the *Play* Three or Four times a Week was common: To *Church* they went to *ſee* and be *ſeen*, and that uſually when *Prayers* were half ended; but to the *Play-houſe* they came in with the firſt, and went out with the laſt; never thinking a *Sermon* too ſhort, or a *Play* too long: In ſhort, both the Sons and Daughters of *State Policy*, were all of their Fathers *Religion*.

Trimmer, the Eldeſt of the three Brothers I have been ſpeaking of, ſtaid longeſt at the *Univerſity*, and according to his Parents deſire was bred a *Divine*: He was accompliſh'd with all endowments requiſite for a *Church-man*, that was to oblige his Kinſwoman *Moderation*, and his Friend St *Whigg*, from whom he expected all his Preferment; and by whom, as ſoon as he had left the *Univerſity*, he was preſented to Two fat *Livings*, tho' during his Studies, he had writ ſtrenuouſly againſt *Pluralities*; but they oblig'd him forcibly to accept of 'em, or loſe their favours for ever: Accordingly our young Doctor, fearful to offend ſuch good Patrons, humbly ſubmitted to their pleaſure. But St. *Whigg* and *Moderation* not ſatisfy'd with this, propos'd to him, That as ſoon as he he was in Poffeffion of the faid Benefices, that he fhou'd take to Wife their Beloved Sifter, *Occafional Conformity*, who was become now the darling of St *Whigg*: This at firft ftuck in the Confcience of *Trimmer*, who wou'd have perfwaded them, that this was no better than *Smock-Symony*, at which St. *Whigg* fell into a great Paffion with him, and demanded a Bond of *Refignation* inftantly; but *Trimmer* taking into confideration, that St. *Whigg* and his Two Sifters Govern'd all before them, and that if he meant to be a *Bifhop*, he muft yield to the Terms they wou'd pleafe to Prefcribe to him; after a fmall *Paufe* he agreed to their Propofal, and took to *have* and to *hold*, for the Term of his Life, the goodly Sifter of St. *Whigg*. This wonderful *Submiffion* of *Trimmer*, was foon reprefented to the Prince as a Meritorious *Act* of *Paffive Obedience*, whereupon he was foon promoted to a *Bifhop-rick*, which he Good Man excepted, purely for the fake of *Peace* and *Quietnefs*. He was not at all chang'd from what he was before, nor lifted up above his Brethren, but a true *Trimmer* ftill, and a conftant pattern to his Flock; his Wife *Occafional Conformity* being much belov'd by him, he was fuch a ftrict Admirer of her, that he never valued enquiring after the *Conformity* of the *Church* as long as fhe liv'd.

CHAP.

CHAP. IV.

Of St. Whigg, *his* Virtue *and Character;
likewise of* Occasional Conformities
Sickness, *and their great Enemy* Jure
Divino.

AND now to return again to St. *Whigg*, his Two Sisters, while living, being of such eminent Quality as you have heard, you can not think that their only Brother St. *Whigg* can want preferment, or sit long without many fair offers for a *great Match*, and many he had: For tho' he was a Man of extraordinary Parts and Accomplishments, yet he never affected *Curiosity* in his *Dress*, or *Nicety* in his *Apparel*, but was always Clerent and Comely; upon that account, all the Gaudy Youthful Ladies who had heard much of his *Fame* and *Virtues*, and had begun to make *Overtures* to him fell off again; because he affecting *State Affairs*, they fear'd he might have too much *Gravity* in him, which was not agreeable to their Light and Frolicksome Humours.

He had a great resemblance both of his *Father* and *Mother*, and was counted a Circumspect Judicious Person, considering every thing to *Admiration*; yet even amidst all this Wisdom, he thought it not below him to advise both *Moderation* and *Occasional Conformity*,

formity, especially in difficult cafes of *State Affairs*, he wou'd be sure to confult with them, becaufe they knew more of the Secrets of the Court than ever St. *Whigg* was let into but through them; neither did he ever repent hearkning to their Advife, for he always found by experience, that their Counfel was always the moft fuccefsful. He was a Man of deep infight into matters of concernment either for *Church* or *State*; but he was never biafs'd by *Self-Intereft* and his Private *Paffions*, notwithftanding he was very watchful what was like to be the Iffue of things, and accordingly always advis'd what was moft for the Intereft of his Friend. He was univerfally admired among the *Mob* above any Mortal Creature, and never had an Enemy powerful enough to hurt him but *Jure Divino*, which was his fworn *Foe*.

Jure Divino was defcended of a Noble Family, and as Ancient as any in the World: He was a Man known far and near for his excellent Education, his great Proficiency, admirable Parts, and *Incredible Travels*; his Life was Irreprovable, and his *Devotion Inimitable*: In his Younger years he had been of a Hot and Fiery Temper, but as he grew Elder, he became more Mild and Moderate; and as he chang'd his *Climate*, fo he chang'd his *Difpofition*, and was quite another Man. He had bin once of that Opinion, that no fort of Men ought to be more feverely *Animadverted* on, and dealt with, than thofe who

D   Diffented

dissented from the *Religion* and *Rites* of their *Forefathers*; and wou'd but Authority pass Acts severe enough for Suppression of such, by *Banishments*, *Bonds*, *Imprisonments*, or *Death*, he wou'd be the Man that wou'd see them put in *Execution*, which he also did, judging it the best Service he cou'd do *God* and his *Country*; thereupon he haled many into *Prisons*, and compell'd them to *abjure*, *Recant*, and Blaspheme, or *suffer* and *dye*.

But after this Treatment, I say, he was quite of another Mind, and became the most complaisant and obliging Person in the World. So that he struck up a Friendship with *Moderation*, till St. *Whigg*, by his *Politick Designs*, broke it quite off, by marrying her to *State Policy*, an avow'd Enemy to *Jure Divino*, who afterwards had, by *Extremity*, a *Bastard Daughter*, call'd *Low-Church*, which afterwards growing very *fair* and *beautiful*, St. *Whigg* fell in love with, and married her. About this time a great *Delirium*, or sort of *Distraction*, seiz'd upon *Occasional Conformity*, which rais'd a mighty Rupture betwixt *Trimmer* her Husband and *Jure Divino*: *Trimmer* justify'd whatever his Wife said or did, and call'd in *Whigg* and *State Policy* to his Assistance, who were so zealous in the matter, to vindicate their Sister's Failings, that *Moderation* run quite Mad. The *Physicians* who were sent for, were at their Wits end when they saw her; they perceiv'd her Trouble lay deeper, and concluded by all

Con-

Conjectures they cou'd make, it was some inward Vexation or Grief oppress'd her, and being much solicited by them, whether it was so or no, she confess'd at last, it was so indeed, and that she was much troubled in *Mind,* and cou'd get no *Rest.*

It was about her former Course of Life; especially she said, one thing lay heavy upon her above all others, which they were long e'er they cou'd get out of her; yet she was observ'd by them that *watch'd* with her, sometimes between sleeping and waking, to mutter to her self, and they cou'd over-hear her now and then, and her talk was of *Jure Divino,* and many times she wou'd start of a sudden, and look a *Gast,* and bid the *By-Standers* look about, and tell her if they saw any thing, and sometimes wou'd ask them, if they saw not *Jure Divino* there? Once she lay as in a *Trance*; at another time she wou'd cry out of her self, and her former Miscarriages, saying, Ah! vile *Occasional Conformity!* Ah! sinful Wretch *Occasional Conformity!* And once she told one of her Maids, That *Jure Divino* had appear'd to her in her sleep, all cloth'd in *White,* and with a smiling Countenance ask'd her, What Reason she had to be so *bitter* an *Enemy* to him, who had never done her Wrong in all his Life? He told her, he was sent to admonish her to repent, and amend her Ways, and then she wou'd be a happy Women.

This *Apparition*, as she was perswaded it was, run much in her Mind, and she wou'd often say, her Sister *Moderation*, and her Brother *Whigg*, had been more in the Fault than her self; but a little after this ill Fit she prov'd with Child, and when she had gone her Time, she was deliver'd of a Daughter, which her Husband *Trimmer* wou'd have call'd *Mitigation*; but *Occasional Conformity* pleaded hard, that this Child, upon account of her late Trouble in Mind, might be brought up with *Jure Div no*, tho' she once had a Mortal Hatred against him; and she also interceeded with her Husband that if this Daughter liv'd to be bestow'd in Marriage, it might be to one of that Family, which she desir'd above any thing in this World: as being verily perswaded she shou'd then dye in *Peace*.

It fell out also unhappily, and much to the Prejdice of St. *Whigg*, that his Three *Cousin Germans*, by his *Aunt Impudence*, *Pride*, *Rebellion*, and *Disobedience*, had much about this time broke out into an open War, and made seditious Commotions, when all People were in Expectation of *Peace*; and not long after, a bloody Rupture and *Civil Dissentions* commenc'd: But *Jure Divino* zealously watchful, and prudently sollicitous to preserve common *Peace* at Home, held a Suspicious Eye over St. *Whigg* and all his Actions, as mistrusting he had underhand countenanc'd the former, or corresponded with the latter: Nor cou'd
St.

St. *Whigg*'s Demureness secure him from many a harsh Sensure and bitter *Taunt*. Then did *Jure Divino* twit St. *Whigg*, and charge him with *Disaffection*, and often hit him in the Teeth with the *Miscarriages* of his *Kindred*, saying thus to him, *You and your Relations think your selves wiser than all the World besides*; *but had I the Power in my Hands, as I ought to have, I wou'd make you and all your Family Pack up and be gone, or else change your Notes.*

While he was talking at this rate to St. *Whigg*, *Pride* and *Disobedience* enter, and turn *Jure Divino* out of Doors; for they bore a perpetual Hatred to him and all his *Family* and *Acquaintance*; St. *Whigg* endeavour'd to pacifie them with what his Sister *Occasional Conformity* had said to him; but *Pride* and *Disobedience* made answer, they thought he had been a wiser Man, than to heed the idle talk of People that *dream*, or Women in the *Vapours*, as long as he knew what a strange Fellow *Jure Divino* was, of a shrew'd and subtle Wit, and that he was a perfect Monster by Birth, being born with *Teeth* in his Head; that he came laughing into the World, with a *Coal of Fire* in one Hand, and a Sword in the other; that Nature had branded him with a Mark of Distinction, as one they ought to have an utter aversion to, unless they were resolv'd to suffer themselves to be extirpated from the Face of the Earth.

They

They further urg'd, That *Jure Divino* was but too well belov'd, and had many *Virtuous* and *Brave Men*, that were both *powerful* and *trusty Friends* to him; that he was the first *Inventor* of those *Instruments* of *Peace*, that had like to have destroy'd at once their Brother *Rebellion*, had not they Two interpos'd and blown the *Trumpet* of *Sedition*, which sav'd him out of his Hands, and at the same time overthrew their *lawful Soveraign*, who headed his *Party*; but he has since, drawn over many *Deserters*, by his wheedling Allurements of *Peace* and *Happiness*, which we have industriously studied to prevent:

'You know, continu'd they on to St. *Whigg*, 'that he has a working Brain, and is of a 'restless Spirit; skillful to Unite, Preserve 'and Govern, and is the only Enemy we 'dread against *Anarchy* and *Confusion*. We 'have, in vain, set our *Heads* and *Hands* to 'work to destroy Kings, blow up Parliaments, 'lay Cities waste, and *Countries* desolate, spoil '*Churches*, and divide between Prince and 'People, to make and encrease *Parties*, if at 'the latter end we suffer this *Jure Divino* to 'interrupt our Purposes, or share with us in 'the Possession.

I tell thee, Cousin *Whigg*, said *Disobedience*, these *Friends* of thine are of so many several *Complexions* and *Dispositions* of late, as if they had not been born of the same Fathers and Mothers, who were formerly notorious for all manner of *Wickedness* imaginable, and if the Children were but like
them;

them, *nothing cou'd come amiſs to us ; for they were ſuch a Generation, for Swearing, Drinking, Whoring, Ranting, Quarrelling, Fighting, Filching, Stealing, cutting of Purſes, and cutting of Throats, as was not in the World again* : Slighting *Laws, Statutes, Penalties, Stocks, Priſon, Gallows, Death and Hell too.*

Our Friends of old, ſaid Pride, *were the true Spawn of the old Leviathan, profeſs'd Atheiſts, and Deriders of all Religions, of the Sadducean Herd, believing neither Angel, Spirit, Heaven, nor Hell* : *But St.* Whigg *has debauch'd their Principles, made 'em Sneakers after Religion, that are forc'd to invent new Oaths and Devices to palliate their Perjuries* : *This makes us appear little, for we dare not venture at a bold Attempt.* Thus *Pride Catechis'd* St. *Whigg,* till he had made him *Belch* out all his *Scoffs* and *Jeſts,* his *impious Oaths* and *Curſes,* and laſt of all his *fulſome Bawdery* Then he began to tell the Story of his Mothers keeping a Publick Houſe, and of the Education of his Two Siſters.

The youngeſt us'd to ſit at the Door of *Phanatica Porne,* when ſhe liv'd in the Suburbs of *Geneva,* and watch to ſee who went by, and what Paſſengers were fit to be call'd in ; and then ſhe wou'd invite 'em in, to come and make choiſe of a Room, and tell 'em what Entertainment was to be had in the Houſe ; being enter'd, ſhe conveys them preſently into her Mother's Lodging, who for her ſelf was richly adorn'd with *Jewels* taken

out

out of the *Triple Crown*, and her Room was hung with rich Hangings she had brought out of the *Vatican*.

After a short stay there, and a *Collation* given, she desires them to go up Stairs to her Sister *Moderation*'s Lodgings; they found her at her Glass, curiously Curling her Locks, patching her Face, with her *naked Breast* expos'd, and her Chamber all hung round with *lacivious Pictures*; if then any one startled, and thought they had seen enough, and ask'd leave to return, they wou'd all Three tell them there was more to be seen above, and they must not refuse to go up one short Pair of Stairs, and tast of *Occasional Conformity*'s Cup; it was a Guilt *Bowl*, containing in it a clear Liquor, of which whosoever once tasted was intoxicated, and then they wou'd desire to see and know all the *Curiosities* of the Place, and to behold *Occasional Conformity* in her most Charming Dress; she was at this Interview preparing *Bracelets* made of her own Hair, and mixing *Potions* for Guests that she expected: When Strangers saw her the second time, they could not know her, she wou'd be so much alter'd from her first appearing *Modesty*; but then she wou'd come boldly up to them and salute them, offering them the Courtesie of the House, and telling them, they must not refuse to Visit her eldest Sister *Moderation* again, whose other *Apartment* wou'd give them more Content, then all they had yet seen.

Here

Here she sat on a *stately Couch*, in rich taffaray, of *Silk* and *Crimson Sattin*, all adorn'd with broad *Gold Lace*; her Face was new Painted; she was decay'd and wrinkled; but her *Paint* made her look as fair as a Rose with a Mixture of *Lillies:* This was a very spacious fair Room, hung with the richest *Arras*; and you wou'd wonder to see what a *Sideboard* of *Plate* was set out, and what a fair Prospect into all the *Fields* and *Gardens* round about: She presented her Company always, by the Hands of her own Woman, a smiling, witty, young *Jade*, with a *Venice-glass* of *Italian* Wine, and some costly *Sweet-meats!* but under the *Balcony* was a close *Trap-door*, discern'd but by few, over a *deep Ditch*, into which, after a little amorous Discourse, or a short wanton Dalliance, *Pharatica Porne*, with the Help of her Two Daughters, us'd to throw her Guests headlong, after they had usually stript 'em of all they had about them. Few or none, that ever I heard of, that came once into Madam *Porne*'s Clutches, ever came back again, or were seen alive; only one escap'd once, to make Relation of their Entertainment: And he said he was fain to steal out at a Back-door which he found lock'd, but exerting all his Strength he burst it open, and then came down a narrow Pair of *Stairs*, very steep and dark, which few were able to find, and so got away, resolving never to come more there; For, said he, had I stay'd longer, or attempted to go

E back

back the same Way I came, I had certainly been snapt: He ever after call'd my Mother and Two Sisters, *the Three fatal Sisters*, and warn'd all his Acquaintance not to come near them. This Confession of his Family Pride and *Disobedience* extorted from St.*Whigg*, in order to please their vitiated Palates, who began now to hug and extol him as their dearest Friend and best Ally.

CHAP.

CHAP. V.

Of St. Whigg*'s Marriage with* Low-Church, *the* Baſtard Daughter *of* Jure Divino, *with an account of their Two* Daughters, Schiſm *und* Faction, *and the Troubles he had with them:* His Separation *from* Low-Church, *and Marriage with* Mitigation, *his own* Neece.

NOW to return to the *Marriage* of St. *Whigg*; it muſt be obſerv'd that his Siſter *Moderation,* ſome time before wou'd fain have marry'd him at *Court*, to one of their own *Rank*, now a *Privy Councellor*'s Daughter, as knowing well how much good more he might do, being aſſiſted by another *Privy Councellor* in his own Boſom. *Trimmer* and *Double* were as earneſt for this as ſhe cou'd be for their Hearts; but finding his Inclinations fix'd another way, they deſiſted from their *Sollicitations*; but then again, they were diſtracted to renew them, when they heard that his Intentions were to marry *Low-Church*, a Baſtard Child of *Jure Divino*'s, their inveterate Enemy. They were ſenſible that this *Alliance* with St. *Whigg* wou'd render *Abortive* all their *Projects* to deſtroy *Jure Divino*, *Root* and *Branch*. But notwithstanding all their Endeavours on all Hands, S*t Whigg*, in a little time after, was married to her, and they liv'd at firſt very happily together, that it became the Wonder of the neighbouring *Gentry* and *Clergy*, and every body admir'd at this *Prodigy*, that St. *Whigg*, whoſe Opinions where once thought ſo widely different, ſhou'd uſe any thing that belong to *Jure Divino* with that Candour and Reſpect.

After the uſual time of *Women*'s Gravitation, his Wife was brought ſafely to Bed of Two Daughters, as his Mother had produc'd the like before When theſe Children was born, they look'd both very beautiful and promiſing, ſo that there was great Rejoicing among the whole Family of St. *Whigg*, nor did *Jure Divino* repine at ſo fair a Birth: But as the Children grew up in Years, they grow monſtrouſly deform'd, that it was impoſſible to tell which was the *ugliest*. This created many Miſunderſtandings betwixt the *Father* and *Mother*, they each reproach'd the other, with vile Reflections. St. *Whigg* told his Wife, the Children were only ugly in Body, a her Father *Jure Divino* was in his Mind; of vicious and debauch'd Principles, that had contaminated the Blood of his Children; beſides, ſhe was of a ſpurious Iſſue, and this was a Curſe upon her, and her *Posterity*. On the other hand, *Low-Church* reflected on her *Husband*, and ſaid, that his *Mother* and their whole *Kind* were common

mon *Proſtitutes*, and that this Curſe upon their Children, was tranſmitted naturally, by the *vitiated Seed* of the *Father*, which muſt needs be full of all Corruption, becauſe it was a plain Mixture of every thing that was Pernicious, and had been ſo *propagated* from one *Generation* to another.

Theſe Diſputes betwixt 'em encreas'd daily, as the Children grew up, that in a little time they became a publick Nuſance to the Neighbourhood, by their perpetual Brawling and Diſturbances, till at laſt St. *Whigg* grew infinitely fond of theſe two *Succubuſſes*, which every body that was aware of 'em in the Street wou'd ſhun; for they were as *Ill-condition'd* as they were *ugly*, and wou'd certainly make Miſchief, if any Perſon by Accident ſtood to talk with them, tho' they had never ſeen them before: Nor did theſe Two Creatures want *Subtilty* or *Stratagem*, to draw People into their Snares; for St. *Whigg* had taught 'em the perfect *Art* of *Cant* and *Diſſimulation*. Whoever was credulous, or apt to take things upon Truſt, was ſure to be deceiv'd by them, for they were *egregious Lyars* at the ſame time. No body in the World pretended to more *Sanctity* or *Moral* Honeſty. *Schiſm* wou'd be always *Canting* about *Religion* and *Liberty of Conſcience*, which ſhe was a great *Stickler* for: While *Faction*, the younger was a mighty ſetter up for *Politicks*; ſhe wou'd talk all Day of *News*, and make ſtrange kind of *Reflections* ſometimes, becauſe ſhe ſaid, there

there was no such things as *Kings* and *Kingdoms* in the World, no longer than such a *Liberty* and *Property* was maintain'd, as allow'd her to do what she pleas'd when she had a Mind to it.

By these and such like *Artifices* they brought their Parents to a happy Agreement again with one another, and they both seem'd doatingly fond, on these Two damnable Daughters of *Iniquity*, which afterwards wrought such *Mischief* in the World. At the same time *Jure Divino* griev'd inordinately, at the Course of Life pursu'd by his two Grandaughters, *Schism* and *Faction*, he attempted all the ways in the World, to reclaim them, but to no purpose; for they were naturally bent to all those kind of Vices they follow'd, and their *Parents* encourag'd them in it. *Jure Divino* made Application at Court, to have them punish'd; but found his *Solicitations* were vain, as long as *State Policy*, their *Unkle*, sat at the Helm of *Government*. Afterwards he addres'd himself to *Double*, who was now advanc'd to the highest Post of the Law, thinking his Character was so clear in the World, that he wou'd not sully it, in denying him a common Piece of Justice he might have claim'd of a profes'd Enemy: *Double* made him a great many more Promises than the rest had done, and gave him the Satisfaction of seeing him oftener than *Jure Divino* desir'd; but at last assur'd him, it was not in his *Power* to punish the Children of St. *Whigg*,

who

who was greater than himſelf, and above the reach of his *Court* to take *Cogniſance* of: He told him *Friendly*, the only way to reach St. *Whigg* or his *Family*, was to apply himſelf to his *Aunt Impudence*, who govern'd all the reſt with an Arbitrary Sway; but *Jure Divino* having a more than ordinary Averſion againſt her, took his leave of *Double*, thank'd him for his kind Advice; but told him, he was reſolv'd for the future to ſit ſtill, and be *contented* with things as they were, rather than have any Buſineſs with *Impudence* or any of her *Family* the remaining part of his Life; and ſo left the *Court* and *Kingdom*.

St. *Whigg*'s perfect Reconciliation with his *Wife* had not been long made up, e'er a worſe *Breach* than the firſt broke out, which was irreconcileable; for St. *Whigg* accus'd her with *Adultery*, and *Correſpondence* with her Father *Jure Divino*; upon this Suſpicion nothing wou'd do with the unforgiving Saint, but a *Divorce abſolute*, ſo as to enable him to marry again; nor wanted he *Friends* enough to carry his Point, had it been more difficult than it was. Beſides, on the other Hand he met with no Oppoſition; for he had ſo ſubdued *Low-Church*, that ſhe had not a Friend wou'd appear for her againſt St. *Whigg*, who had ſo wheedled all her Relations to his Intereſt, that they took againſt her, and were ſtrait for packing her away again to *Jure Divino*; but he having retir'd out of the *Kingdom*, ſhe was order'd to an *Hoſpital*, and had a *Penſion*
ſettled

settled upon her, only during her good Behaviour to her former Lord and Master, and the future Pleasure of St. *VVhigg*.

As soon as this Point was gain'd, and *Low-Church* reduc'd to the utmost Extremity of contempt and dishonour; that nothing might be wanting to sink her to the lowest *Dispair*, he publickly makes his Addresses to his own Neece, *Mitigation*: At first, indeed, the Proposal shock'd *Trimmer*, her Father; and *Moderation* her self, had much ado to dispence with it; but *Occasional Conformity* soon comply'd with the Request; and tho' the *Canons* threatned St. *VVhigg* with a *second Divorce*, he was resolv'd to stand their *Fire*, knowing well the *Interest* of his new Spouse *Mitigation* wou'd bring him off, if his own *Power* shou'd fail him, which had hitherto prov'd *Invincible*; since *Jure Divino* had fallen before him, and none of her *Family* since, dare own themselves publickly to be his Enemies.

Notwithstanding this barbarous Usage of St. *Whigg* to *Low Church*, she made her greatest Efforts to seek for *Justice* against this cruel Husband of hers, not imagining but she shou'd find *Friends* to vindicate her *Injur'd Innocence*. But Alas! where are naked *Virtue's Friends* to be found! All her old Acquaintance were grown Stangers to her; and what went nearest to her Heart, *Moderation*, which us'd to flatter her with strange *Romantick Felicities* in her *Marriage* with St. *VVhigg*; she that went formerly to support and countenance her in every

every thing now inftead of comforting her, reviled her for pretending to Match with her *Brother*, whom all the G*r*andees of the *Court* follicited for their Son-in-law: Nay, and what ftill added to her *Afflictions*, her *Father* was as it were, forc'd from his *Native Country*, or at leaft oblig'd to feek an Inglorious *Retirement*, and the reft of her Old Friends and *Acquaintance* were under *Clouds*, and nothing appear'd to 'em but a *melancholly Profpect* of *Misfortunes*.

At laft, after much *Pain* and *Trouble*, fhe met with one *Friend* among the *Multitude*, and that was one fhe had highly difoblig'd in her *Marriage* with St. *VVhigg*, this was one *Philotheos*, a Man that often incurr'd the Difpleafure of great Men, in folliciting for *Innocent Afflicted Perfons*: For being fomewhat plain, and a little fmart in *Reproving Low-Church*, fhe was rather for fitting down with the ill Ufage of St. *VVhigg*, then proceed with fuch a fevere *Reprover*. However, *Philotheos* being concern'd for her in Point of *Honour* and *Confcience*, and for the *Publick Welfare*, cou'd not for his Life fit ftill, but prefents a *Humble* and *Modeft Petition* in her behalf, which was this, That they might come to a fair hearing, and when Matters fhou'd be rightly underftood, if fhe was found an Offender, he defir'd no favour for her; he defir'd no more, and expected at leaft fhe might have been call'd in and fpoken to, or her *Petition* read however. But when no

Admitance cou'd be obtain'd for her, and inftead thereof, *Taunts* and *bitter Reproaches*, fent after, and fhe was told withal, that if fhe mov'd any further, fhe fhou'd be *fecur'd*: She took it fo to Heart, that fhe never enjoy'd her felf afterwards, nor had any delight to go abroad, but liv'd retir'd in her private *Lodgings*, and gave her felf to her *Devotions*.

A little time after St. *Whigg*'s Marriage with *Mitigation*, News was brought to *Court*, that *Moderation* departed the fame Day that *Low-Church*'s *Petition* was rejected: It was reported fhe dy'd a great Penitent, and left ftrict charge on her *Death-bed*, to all her Friends, that Intereft fhou'd be made to recall *Jure Divino*, and to reinftate 'em in their former Poffeffions; but *Trimmer*, *Double*, and *State Policy* no fooner receiv'd this News, but it ftruck them to the very *Heart*, that they were fcarce able to out-live their Sifter *Moderation*; never were fuch *Lamentations* known among *Relations*. Now *Court*, *City* and *Country* were full of *Grief*, for the *lofs* of fuch an Eminent Perfon, that was the very Spring of all the Motions of the *State* at *Home*, particularly were her neareft Kindred rul'd without Controul on the contrary; this as much rejoic'd *Pride*, *Rebellion*, and *Difobedience*, as it had mortify'd *Trimmer* and *State Policy*, who had fpread the Character of *Moderation* all over the Kingdom, fo that fhe was univerfally mourn'd for, by all that had any concern in the Adminiftration of Affairs. She had

been

been generally applauded and talk'd of all the *Island* over, as an excellent Subject, that cou'd live under any *Prince*, and therefore she was bewail'd by Man, Woman and Child, young and old, simple and gentle, because they were all possess'd with an Opinion, that she had no Interest but the *Publick Good*, falsly so call'd, and desir'd Favour and Protection only for such, as shou'd be judg'd worthy to live in any well-govern'd State in the World: And they lamented her the more, because she desir'd, on her Death-bed, to have *Jure Divino* and his Family taken into favour again.

Never was any *Mourning* greater than this, or any Persons recovery more desir'd then this *Ladies*: And what is very remarkable, is this, tho' it be against the *Religion* profess'd in this *Country*, to put up *Prayers* for the dead, yet all the *Friends* of *Moderation* made publick Intercession for the Peace of her Soul, and her *quick Return*, of which they have a stedfast *Faith* and full Expectation to this Day. Nay, so *Idolatrous* were they grown on this Score, that seldom any of them came near her *Tomb*, but they be-dew'd it with their *Tears*; so that at last several of them became so *superstitious* as to think she was *risen* again, and declar'd to the World, insomuch that the whole Country was fill'd with the Noise of it, and the common People receiv'd it as *faithfully*, if not with more Assurance than ever they did the *Articles* of their *Creed*.

F 2   CHAP.

CHAP. VI.

Of the wonderful Change wrought in State Policy, *and his Defection afterwards.*

Upon the Death of *Moderation,* State Policy observing the universal Grief and Dejection of the People, it made a strange Impression on his *Mind,* and he began to think what wou'd be the Consequence of all those *unnatural Proceedings* they had made use of against *Jure Divino.* He began now to make enquiry, and think with himself what able and discreet Person there was in his Neighbourhood to whom he might unbosom himself, and was told, there liv'd not far from him a choice and prudent Man, nam'd *Philotheos,* one well experienc'd in *Cases of Conscience* and Perplexities of *Mind,* a chearful and comfortable old Man he was, and yet one that wou'd never flatter you, but speak the *Plain Truth.*

State *Policy* had never been acquainted with him before, tho' they had liv'd not far one from another; for he always look'd upon him as a *four, discontented Fellow*; but sending for him, he came directly; upon sight of whom, State *Policy* was ready immediately to rise off his *Couch,* and fall down upon his Knees to him. *Philotheos* ask'd him chearfully, How he did? And, what was his Grief? He presently con-

confess'd he had been a grievous Sinner, and had much offended; but one thing there was, which he had hitherto conceal'd, but now he wou'd hide nothing from him: One thing there was that troubled him more than all the rest, He had been a bitter Enemy to *Jure Divino*; but now he saw plainly he had been much mistaken in him, and fear'd he had too much to answer for his *Uncharitableness*. He had always look'd upon *Jure Divino* with an evil Eye, as if he had been the vilest Creature alive, and thereupon had hated him to Death; but now he was quite and clear of another Mind, and did think he was as good a Man as liv'd, and the most innocent; nay, he saw plainly he was a better Christian than himself, wishing withal, that when they both came to dye, he might exchange Places with *Jure Divino*. This and much more he confest, and then gush'd out when he mention'd these things.

Another thing he charg'd himself withal, which he thought made him more inexcusible, and he said he had never thought of it till now, and that was this: He had been formerly under the Hands of cruel *Oppressors*, and cou'd not help himself; and indeed he had hard Measure, but it was not from the Hands of *Jure Divino*, nor any of his *Friends*, who cou'd only pity him, and were troubled to see it. At that time he promis'd, and made a solemn Vow, that if ever he shou'd come out of his *Sufferings*, he had learn'd to pity *Suffer-*

ers as long as he liv'd, and ſhou'd never countenance *Violence* again: Yet ſince he had been in that good Condition he now enjoy'd, tho' *Jure Divino* had not been backward to contribute his beſt Aſſiſtance for his and the common Benefit, he had both forgot him and his own former *Vows* and *Promiſes*: And here he burſt out into Tears afreſh.

Philotheos ſeeing him in ſuch an *Agony*, fell to comforting of him, and told him, he had been much to blame for his former *Violence*, but ſeeing he was now ſo true a *Penitent*, and ſo much chang'd in his *Mind* as he declar'd, he advis'd him not to be afraid, his *Caſe* was not yet *deſperate*; and to comfort him, he told him further, That he had frequently met with the like *Caſes* before. The greateſt Princes had been drawn aſide ſometimes, as he had been, as *Darius* and *Ahaſuerus*, whoſe good Natures had been wrought upon, by the ſollicitation of ſome *Miſ-informers*, to paſs ſome *Acts*, ſevere enough, againſt ſome of *Jure Divino*'s *Anceſtors:* Yet upon further enquiry and ſatisfaction of their *Error*, they have check'd thoſe Proceedings, and repeal'd ſuch Acts; nay, afterwards they have receiv'd into higheſt favour ſuch, as by *Miſrepreſentation*, they had been exaſperated againſt; nor was it ever imputed to them as a Note of *Ignominy*, that they had reſcinded ſuch *Acts*, but is the brighteſt *Star* of *Glory* that ſhines in their *Hiſtory*. The like Converſion, I hope, ſaid *Philotheos*, will happen to you, whoſe

former

former Days, by your own *Confeſſion* have been like theirs; and if you continue in this good Mind, you will no doubt receive the ſame Praiſe and Encomiums they have done in all ſucceeding Ages.

But to ſhew you the *Unconſtancy* of *State Policy*'s *Reſolutions*, not long after this *Qualm* of *Conſcience*, the *Court* prefer'd him to a *higher Poſt*, which at once deſtroy'd all his *good Reſolutions*, and made him as bitter an Enemy to *Jure Divino* as ever he was before.: The Loſs of *Moderation*, and her *laſt Charge* to him, was now all quite forgot and laid aſide. He found by late *Experience*, that St. *Whigg*'s and *Mitigation*'s Intereſt, had top'd upon all that went before them, therefore he was reſolv'd no longer to entertain any Thoughts of what had paſs'd betwixt him and *Philotheos*; but at once proſecute the good *Fortune* that had befall'n him, through the *Meditation* of St. *Whigg*, whom he knew wou'd never be reconcil'd to *Jure Divino*, or any of his *Race* again. The *Coals* of his Anger were now blown up to too high a *Pitch*, to end in any thing but *Aſhes*; and his Temper was ſo implacable when provok'd, that he never once forgave any that offended him; That made him appear terrible to his Adverſaries, that the Fame of St. *Whigg*'s unforgiving Temper was as ſhocking to his *Enemies*, as the Declaration of *No Quarter* is to an *Army* at the onſet of a Battel.

This

This begot in *State Policy* new *Resolutions* of exerting himself more vigorously than heretofore: In order to which he enter'd into a fresh *Alliance* with St. *Whigg*, That for the future they shou'd not suffer *Jure Divino* once to set Footing in the *Kingdom* more; but that a *Proclamation* shou'd be issued out, to forbid all Persons whatsoever from holding any Correspondence with him; and for his *Friends, Abettors* or *Adherents*, that they shou'd be us'd with the severest Rigour, in order to weary them either out of their *Principles*, or their *Country*: Accordingly *Spies* and *Informers* were plac'd in all *Publick Houses*, and in every Corner of the Streets, to betray such as were too *open hearted*, and so free as to own themselves related to *Jure Divino*; by which Method a great many *innocent* and *well-meaning Persons* were brought into Troubles, and others entirely ruin'd and undone, which caus'd St. *Whigg* to triumph every Day more than other, over those unfortunate Wretches, who were forced to submit to an *Arbitrary Power* he had extorted from them, and at the same time exercised over them, with a strange insulting kind of *Barbarity*.

CHAP.

CHAP. VII.

What became of Pride, Rebellion *and* Disobedience; *together with a* Digression *of the Authors.*

IT may not be amiss in the last Place, after St. *Whigg's* great Exaltation, to give some Account what became of *Pride, Rebellion* and *Disobedience,* which notwithstanding the great *Oppressions* and *Persecutions* of *Jure Divino,* where by him and his *Interest* very much supprest, and brought under the *Hatches.* *Pride* was of such extream ill Temper, that he was not to be touch'd with any sense of *Honour* or *Conscience,* while his *Antagonist, Jure Divino,* was of a generous Spirit and noble Education, and ever bare a true love to his *Country*; but only he was too *passionate.* *Disobedience* and *Rebellion* on the other side, were of *dogged, surly* and *unquiet Dispositions*; nothing could please 'em, neither could they well tell what they would have; but they always fretted at the *Times,* and their own private Condition.

This *Mischievous Family* always put *Jure Divino* and his *Party* upon their *Guard,* to watch the *perpetual Disturbances* they made, and to prevent their future Designs, which were always *Villainous,* to subvert the very Foundation of Government, and to involve all Mankind in *Anarchy* and *Confusion*; for there was nothing in Nature so monstrous and absurd, that they wou'd not devise and attempt to execute; while their Enemies only, and Men who were watchful for the *Peace* of their *Country*, agreed with their united Forces of *Diligence, Conduct, Courage* and *Concord*, to fall upon them: And they being in a short time up with *Rebellion*, it was the Lot of a *Party* of *Diligences*, to give the first Charge, who scatter'd the Body, and took some of the chief *Heads*, and made them Exmples; and *Conduct* with his *Party*, took some others, while *Courage* and *Concord*, agreed, to the Terror of their Leaders, to send them bound to *Absalom's Oak*, drawn backward in his *Chariot* by his *Mule*, whom when she carried thither, and had left them all safe, hanging between *Heaven* and *Earth* upon a *Three-forked Branch*, went away from under them, leaving them suspended and expos'd to the rude Insult of the *Inclement Air*.

Some of the rest, that were taken stragling, were made to go on *Pilgrimage* a Foot to the *Royal-Oak*, a *Tree* they had a mortal aversion to, upon account of the good Services it had done its *Country* in the Days of their *Forefathers*: And because this *Tree* was somewhat more *August* than the former, they were forc'd to climb, or else be lifted up to it; presently after, the kind Earth, to rid the World

of

of such enormous Wretches, open'd and swallow'd them up.

The *Heads* being thus taken off, the rest submitted, and fell to hard Labour, all, save a few desperate ones, who seeing they could do no *more good on't*, as they call'd *Mischief* and *Wickedness*, fled the *Land*; only some of the younger Children of *Disobedience*, to wit, the *Hectors* and *Bullies*, with some other vicious Persons, remain'd sculking in Corners, and harbour'd in wicked Houses, whom 'tis hop'd may be reclaim'd by the good and wholesome *Laws* of the *Country*; for there are no better by Report any where, if they are duly put in *Execution*; when no Nation in the World, can boast of more *Happiness* and *solid Satisfaction*.

I am not ignorant, that many will look upon all this that hath been said of the St. *Whigg* and his *Family*, of the *Sickness* and *Repentance* of *Moderation*, and the *Transactions* of *Jure Divino*, to be but a *Story*: And for my Part, I shall not go about to impose upon any Man a belief of what is here said, but leave every one to think what he pleases. But in the first Place, it is certain that St. *Whigg* and *Low-Church* made a very unhappy Match, after all the World had given them *Joy*, and wish'd they might live in Prosperity together. 'Tis true, they had Children; but they
prov'd

Prov'd a Curſe to all that wiſh'd 'em *Joy*; Yet their Parents were wonderfully delighted with 'em for a Time, till *Schiſm* and *Faction* made ſuch a *Breach* betwixt them which was never repair'd again all their Lives after. But St. *Whigg* put her away, and took to him *Mitigation*, upon which ſecond *Marriage* he appear'd to be a New Man, and was all Goodneſs to his *Neighbours*; that whenſoever he came abroad, it was obſerv'd there was a freſh breathing of a Spirit of *Love* all over, as if ſome gentle *Zephuris* had blown away all the former Clouds and Storms, and preſented him with a milder Air; nay, the very Content of his *Heart* and *Hope* was legible in his Countenance.

But what the ſecret Cauſes of the *Alteration* and *Reconciliation*, between *Jure Divino* and *Moderation* were, is too deep a Miſtery for me to penetrate into; Only I ſhall relate to you, what were the ſeveral Conjectures of ſeveral Perſons, who would, as they pleas'd, aſſign their ſeveral *Opinions Firſt*, This is not to be conceal'd, That the Inhabitants of that Nation, were a People, beyond any in the World, given to *change* and *alteration*; and that they had taken Notice, after ſome hard Dealing with *Jure Divino*, many Diſaſters had befall'n them, which, tho' it were too high a Preſumption to give the reaſon of, yet it is but fit to take Notice of 'em, as the *Apparition* of ſome Prodigious
Comets

[53]

Comets that amaz'd the *Spectators*, after that *Plague*, *Fire* and *War*, and at the End of all thefe, a *Revolution*, that turn'd all things up-fide down, and plac'd *Moderation* in the room of *Jure Divino*, and made a *second Pope Joan* of her.

Others there were, that afcrib'd this *Reconciliation* to the *Prudence* of the *Prince*, who having obferv'd how patient and filent *Jure Divino* had been, under his Trials, and moreover when fome unquiet Spirits had been formerly ftirring at Home, and during the time of a *War*, that was then afoot with their Neighbours abroad, *Moderation* her felf could not find the leaft *Defect* in him from his wonted conftant Fidelity, thereupon fhe interceeded with the Prince; her felf, to bring him out of his Troubles, and the Difgrace he had lain under, for a falfe Accufation. Thus after *Moderation* had become his *Patron*, *Friend* and *Advocate*, fhe dy'd, and left him to the Mercy of her Brother *Whigg*, who has vow'd an everlafting Hatred againft him, and every Branch of his detefted Race.

FINIS.

The Life and Adventures of Captain John Avery

Anonymous

Bibliographical note:
This facsimile has been made from a copy in the British Museum (1204.c.5)

THE
Life and Adventures
OF
Capt. *John Avery*,

THE

Famous *English* Pirate, (rais'd from a Cabbin-Boy, to a King) now in Poffeffion of

MADAGASCAR:

BEING

A Succinct Account of his Birth, Parentage, Education, Misfortunes, and Succeffes, *viz.* His feizing the Government on Board the *Refolution* and *Nonfuch* Men of War. The Reafons why he quitted that Service, for that of the Merchants. His putting to Sea in a Merchant Ship, where he drew in the Crew to turn Pirates with him. His failing to *Jamaica*, where he difpos'd of the Ship's Cargo. His taking a large Ship, worth above a Million Sterling, belonging to the Great *Mogul*, with his Grand-Daughter on Board, (who was going to be Marry'd to the King of *Perfia*) attended by a great Retinue of Ladies. His Marriage with the faid Princefs, and his Men with her Retinue. The Methods he took to eftablifh himfelf. His Wealth, Strength, and Acquifitions by Sea and Land. His Character. The feveral Overtures he has made to return to his Obedience. A Defcription of the Country; with its Cuftoms, Manners, *&c.*

Written by a Perfon who made his Efcape from thence, and faithfully extracted from his Journal.

London, Printed: And Sold by *J. Baker*, at the Black-

THE
PREFACE.

AS Prefaces *are, necessary where the Credit of any Memoir is liable to be called in Question, so it may* not *be improper to give the Reader one at this Juncture, who, from the many Impositions of this Nature, will be apt to suspend his Belief concerning Things so remotely transacted, and Persons so obscure and imperceptible in their Practice.* Who is this pretended Author, that made his Escape from *Madagascar? says one.* How came he to be let into the Captain's inmost Secrets? *cries another; and every one gives himself a Liberty concerning a Writer* that is *juſtly ſaid, by the late Dr.* Sherlock, *to* lie down, *while every Reader takes a Priviledge in cenſuring what he buys, which is really his own by that Purchaſe, and hits him a Kick in the Britch, to make him* exerciſe his Faculty of Feeling.

To gratify ſuch curious Enquiries as theſe, and prepoſſeſs the Publick againſt all manner of ſcrupulous Objections, it is, to know that the Author of this ſmall Treatiſe is one Adrian Van Broeck, *a* Dutch *Gentleman, who, after a very liberal Education at* Leyden, *apply'd himſelf, as Men of the beſt Faſhion in* Holland *do, to the Buſineſs of Trade. This Application, which he made to the Satisfaction of all that he dealt with, made him known to the Governors of the* Dutch Eaſt India Company, *who, in order to encourage ſo much Deſert, made him Supercargo to one of their outward-bound Ships, very richly laden, call'd the* Zealand, *with Letters recommendatory*

The Preface.

tory for a profitable Employ, when he should arrive at Batavia.

But Fortune, *that is not always in Friendship with those who deserve it, suffer'd this Ship to spring a Leak, and founder at Sea, near the Island of* St. Hellena, *tho' the Crew made their Escape in their Pinnaces and Long-Boats; among the rest,* Adrian Van Broeck, *who had lost very considerably of his own by this Disaster, came ashore, and, after Application to the Governor, got another Ship upon the Company's Account, and so made the best of his Way for* Batavia.

Yet, notwithstanding the Danger he had just before escap'd from, and the Treasure this Type of Inconstancy had made the devouring Sea rob him of, he was to fall under another Disappointment more severe than the former, which was, to be intercepted in his Voyage by Pirates, that were some of Capt. Avery's *Band, and, after plundering him of his ready Money,*

Money, which confifted of some thousand Dollars, brought him and his Ship and Company into Madagascar; where, being had before the Captain, to be examin'd about his Circumstances, and the Affairs of Europe, the Captain contracted such an Esteem for him, as not only to offer him a free Residence with him, but such a Share in his new-erected Government, as he should think fit to accept of.

Van Broeck was by no Means to incur his Displeasure and ill Will, by a Denial, wherefore he laid hold of his Offer, and was admitted into his most secret Thoughts, which gave him Occasion to know such a part of these Memoirs, as his Birth, Education, Marriage, &c. which he was not an Eye-Witness to.

But as generous and liberal Spirits cannot long down with dishonourable Practices, so this Gentleman could no longer brook an Abode amongst this Nest of Thieves, than Necessity requir'd quir'd, and laying hold of the English East India *Man*, *whom the Sequel of these Memoirs will tell us to be dismiss'd in Safety, with a Letter to the Governor of* Fort St. George, *he got on Board with his Effects, which consisted of Money which* Avery *had plentifully stor'd him with, by Stealth in the Night-season; and so, after staying some Time in the* English *Settlements, got safely to* Batavia, *where he now lives possess'd of a very good Post, which he was before recommended to.*

What remains after this, is, to answer some Objections which may be made to the Truth of it, from his mentioning nothing of this in the Body of the Memoirs; and this may be done by referring the Reader to the best Writers of this kind, such as Cæsar *in his* Commentaries, *&c. who industriously pass over what relates to themselves, unless an absolute Necessity requires it. Besides, it would very much take off from the*
Opinion

The Preface.

Opinion of our *Author's Judgment and Qualifications, to introduce any Thing relating to himself in a History that treats of nothing but unjustifiable Principles and Practices.*

To keep the Reader no longer from entering into the House, by detaining him in the Porch, he has nothing to do, but to go in and make himself welcome; where, tho' he will find no Dainties, or Luxuriance of Stile to feed upon, he'll have that the Gods themselves were pleas'd with at a homely Entertainment at Baucis's *and* Philemon's, *if the Poet faith Truth by his* Super omnia Vultus accessere boni.

THE LIFE
OF
Capt. *Avery.*

AS Truth is more necessary towards enlightening Matters purely Historical, than the Embelishments of Stile, and a naked Simplicity more suits this *Truth*, than those ornamental Advantages which are wanting to set off Falsehoods and Romantick Relations, the Writer of these Memoirs, who is perfectly well known to the Person that gives

Being to 'em, has thought fit to entertain his Reader with none of those Flourishes our modern Annalists and Historians abound with, but, without assuming to himself any of their Airs, lays Things before him without any other Dress, than the Gentleman he is now going to treat of, had when his Mother first brought him into the World.

Capt. *John Avery* was born at *Plymouth*, a noted Sea-port Town in *Devonshire*, in the Year 1653, and rather descended from Parents noted for their Industry, than Birth. His Father had spent several Years of his Life in the Service of the Crown, with his Fellow-Townsman Admiral *Blake*; but meeting with little Encouragement, and finding a total Defection from the Royal Cause in the beginning of the late Civil War, chose rather to abandon his dearest Friend and Country-man, than his Sovereign Lord,

Lord, he betook himself to the Merchants, under whom, by his prudent and careful Demeanor, he got a competent Estate, and the Reputation of a very able Sea-man. His Mother, who had the Care of the young Infant during her Husband's Absence in foreign Parts, was not behind-hand with him in her Industry at Home, but took such Care of the Son as might one Day render him possess'd of the Abilities of the Father; but unfortunately dying while her Husband was at Sea, and her Son in the sixth Year of his Age, left him to the Direction of a Sister of her's, one Mrs. *Norris*, who was an Inhabitant of the same Town with her.

This Aunt of his, who was a Widow, and had no Children of her own, surpass'd the Mother (if it was possible) in Tokens of Affections, and, finding him of a very forward Genius, took such Care of his Education, as was proper for a Child, of whom she had conceiv'd such promising Hopes; and, having put him to School, had the Satisfaction not only of seeing him out-strip those of his own Years, but those that had been born some Years before him. But here, as if Fate pointed out the Grandeur and Wealth which should in Process of Time (unfortunately) arrive at, he gave Indications of such a daring and commanding Genius, as made some of his little School-fellows very uneasy, and give in many Complaints against him for his tyrannical Treatment. Though their Complaints were to no Purpose, Nature had eradicated in him a Thirst of Empire; and Obedience to his Superiors was as little consonant to his Character, as a moderate and obliging Behaviour to his Inferiors.

The Master heard and saw all this, and chastis'd him to no Purpose. At last the Father return'd Home, and being content with the Fortunes he had happily acquir'd, wisely resolv'd to tempt the Inconstancy of the Seas no more, but to cast Anchor in a Port that would render him secure from all the Dangers the Winds and Waves had before threaten'd him with. To put these Resolutions in Practice, he purchas'd upwards of eight Score Pounds a Year near *Plymouth*, at a Place call'd *Cut-Down*, a sort of an Eminence over-looking an Arm of the Sea, which, by various Mæanders and Windings, runs several Miles into the Country, and takes its Name from a Mountain or Down, which at once swells above, and defends it from the Insults of tempestuous Weather.

Here the brave old Man took up his Residence, and after having liv'd liv'd to fee the Royal Family reſtor'd in the Perſon of that Auguſt Monarch, King *Charles* the IId, and his Country deliver'd from the Uſurpations it had tyrannically labour'd under for many Years, ſung his *Nunc dimittis*, and gave up his Soul, *March* the 14th 1663, into the Hands of him that gave it him.

Now was our young Pirate juſt entering into the eleventh Year of his Age, and once more under the immediate Care of his Aunt, who was appointed for his Guardian, together with Mr. *Bartholomew Knowles*, a Sea-faring Perſon, who was equally rich with old *Avery*, but not equally honeſt, as the Sequel will give us to underſtand. His Aunt liv'd with him under the Capacity of a Truſtee for about four Years, when being of a very great Age, ſhe gave Way to the Declenſions of Nature, and paying Obedience to the Laws of Mortality,

tality, left this World, and him possefs'd of 500 *l.* more than he had before her Deceafe.

Mr. *Knowles* being now fole Executor, and thofe Impediments remov'd, by his Aunt's Death, which hinder'd him from putting thofe evil Defigns in Practice, which he had long projected; what does he to compafs them, but by giving Way to thofe Inclinations he faw moft predominant in his *Ward*, encourage him in his Defires to go aboard a Fleet of Men of War that was then going to fuppreſs the Neft of Pirates at *Algiers*.

Avery, for his Part, took this as an Earneft of his Indulgence, and being vefted with the Character of a Reformade by the King's Letter, he fet Sail from *Plymouth* with the Squadron that was order'd out for the Purpofes before mention'd; where we fhall leave him, to fee

how

how his Guardian bestow'd his Time in his Absence, who husbanded it as well as Villany could instruct him, by the following Method:

There was a neighbouring Attorney, with whom he had contracted an intimate Acquaintance, (I will not say Friendship, for that's an Appellation no ways familiar to Men of evil Dispositions and Characters) and who had as true a Taste as himself of Things forbidden by the Laws of God and Man. This Backslider, *in noverint Universis*, knew as well how to forge Deeds, as his Brother in Iniquity how to persuade him to it, and it took not up much Labour, but Conveyances were made, and other Instruments drawn, which entitled *Knowlss* to the Possession of the Estate at *Cat-Down*, exclusive of the lawful Proprietor. A hundred Pounds for his Pains, removed

ved all Difficulties, and neither the Violation of Things sacred and civil after such a delicate Morsel, put the least Rub in his Way. As for the five hundred Pounds, he had no manner of Consultation about getting of them into his Hands, they were already in 'em, and a good round Bill of Charges would soon make him Master of that Sum, without any Fear of the Equity of his *Ward*'s Pretences.

In the mean while, young *Avery* shews an uncommon Readiness in the Practice of Maritime Affairs, and not only gets into the Esteem of the Officers of his Majesty's Ship the *Resolution*, which he serv'd aboard, but of the Commadore Rear Admiral *Lawson*, and having exerted an extraordinary Vigour and Sprightliness while *Algiers* was reduc'd to Reason by the Terror of the *English* Navy, begg'd of his Captain to let him serve in the

the same Quality as he did in his Ship, aboard another Vessel that was order'd with three more to be detach'd for the *West Indies*, where the *Spaniards* began to be troublesome to our foreign Plantations; which was immediately granted him, as a Token of the good Will that Commander bore him, and an Encouragement to his future Progress in the Art of Navigation.

But I must not carry him from aboard the *Resolution*, to the *Nonesuch*, (for that was the Ship he was to go to the *Indies* in) before I give the remarkable Occurrence which claims a Share in this History, which is this; It being a Custom for the Reformades, especially those which are most in the good Graces of the Commanding Officer, to dine with the Captain, it was his good Fortune to be one of 'em, while they were taking in Provision at the Port of *Cadiz*, and the second Lieu-

Lieutenant of the Ship being then invited alfo to Table; they fell to Gaming, as is ufual, for want of other Diverfion, after Dinner, and our young Tarpawlin had the Fortune to ſtrip this Officer of the ready Money he was Mafter of, and would not play with him after, as he was defir'd, upon Honour. This enrag'd the Lieutenant to the laſt Degree, who vow'd Revenge, not being able to accomplifh it in the Captain's Prefence, where no Breach of the Peace was to be committed, and the profoundeſt Refpect was due. He therefore took Occafion next Morning to fhew his Refentment by a Baſtinado, for a pretended Neglect in the Reformade's not doing his Duty; who not being able to brook a Blow that was given him fo undefervedly, having watched the Lieutenant afhore, got Leave of his Officer likewife to have the Boat mann'd out and go afhore, where he found his Antagoniſt; and

after

after calling him to Account for Satisfaction, had it in wounding him in several Places, for which he was confin'd at his returning on Board again, for some Time, but afterwards dismiss'd with Applause for his gallant Behaviour, when his Captain came to be inform'd of the true State of the Case.

We have no Room to question, but this fortunate and daring Adventure flush'd him with Expectations of Success in his future Encounters, and gave Additions to a Courage that stood in need of no Access to it. But to be as concise as we can in our Narration, without any Digressions by Way of Remarks, let it suffice, that we bring him in the Commadore's Ship before *Port Royal* in *Jamaica*; where, being of an active Genius, while the Vessels of War were careening, he grew impatient of some other Exploit, and put himself aboard a Buccaneer, who was going in Queſt of Plunder, and was ſo fortunate as to return to *Jamaica* with ſome Ingots of Gold and Silver to his Share; but as he was of an expenſive Temper, it did not long ſtay with him, but went among the Inhabitants, to make appear, that he was not only a perfect Sailor in the Knowledge of Things relating to the Sea, but alſo very readily vers'd in the Practices of thoſe that uſe it, upon the Account he was then embark'd in.

Here he ſtay'd cruizing and ſecuring the Commerce in thoſe Seas, for the Space of two Years, when the Commodore being recall'd home, he was oblig'd to ſet Sail for his Country; at which he was no ſooner arriv'd, but he found his Guardian dead, and himſelf diſpoſſeſs'd not only of his Eſtate, but Aunt's Legacy, by a pretended Deed of Conveyance, and Bill of Charges. Whom to have Recourse to in these Extremities, he knew not. At last, having receiv'd the Pay that was due to him from the Ship, he commenc'd a Suit against *Knowles* his Executors, but all to no Purpose; for what by the Treachery of his own Lawyers, and what by the Pre-possession of the Judges in his Adversary's Favour, he found himself brought under the Necessity of going to Sea again, by losing his Favour.

And here an Opportunity offer'd for his being employ'd, and revenge himself upon his Country's Enemies, for the Perfidies of his pretended Friends. King *Charles* the IId had declar'd War against the *Dutch* for several Incroachments on his Royal Prerogative, and a Fleet was going to Sea to do his Majesty Justice for those Injuries. Among the Rest that made Application

cation for Preferment on this Occasion, *Avery* was one that attended the Board of Admiralty; but his Fortunes being lost, his former Favours were vanish'd also; and though he had serv'd so long under a more genteel Character, he found himself oblig'd to submit to a Foremast-man's Place a board the *Edgar*, where he continu'd during that whole War in no other Capacity, than having the Satisfaction of being serviceable to his King and Country.

When both Parties were weary of fighting, they began then more seriously to enter into the Causes of their Enmity; which not being thought sufficient to justify it on either Side, occasion'd a Treaty of Peace between two Nations, that had been beaten enough to make 'em take Care how they fell together by the Ears again for the future. This returns our Champion back

back again of Courſe to the Place of his Nativity, where having ſome Intereſt, though he had none with the Conncil to his Royal Highneſs the Duke of *York*, then Lord High Admiral, he prevail'd with ſome Merchants of *Totnes* and *Plymouth*, upon a Ship's being bound for the *Weſt Indies*, to be her Commander, and was ſo fortunate in her, as to perform ſeveral Voyages for his Owners with all imaginable Succeſs.

The Places he traded to for the Merchants, were chiefly the Leeward Iſlands; but his Genius being active and enterprizing, he made bold to ſail farther, and went to the Bay of *Campeachy*, where he cut down a conſiderable Quantity of Log-wood, traffick'd with the *Spaniar ls*, and return'd Home with a very rich Cargo.

The Merchants look'd upon him as a lucky and bold Commander, his Courage had been try'd upon several Occasions, and his Conduct been render'd irreproachable, thro' the many happy Results of it, as all his Behaviour was with as much Gallantry as could be expected from the most resolute Sailor on the Ocean. Nor did he, by several other Acts of Prudence and Justice, miss of their Esteem who trusted and employ'd him; for indeed, to speak impartially of this Captain, he had been worthy of a very great Character, if he had made Use of those excellent Qualities, which he was in an eminent Manner Master of, for the Benefit of his Country, as he afterwards manag'd them for its Disadvantage.

'Tis with a great deal of Address and Difficulty, that some very able Politicians make themselves beloved and esteem'd by those they have

have a Design upon; but Capt. *Avery*, without the least Uneasiness, had the Art of gaining the Affections of the Mariners, and shewing his Authority, without weakening their Inclinations for his having the Exercise of it; nay, our better Sort of Tarpawlins, that lay'd Claim to more distinguishing Apprehensions, view'd their Images, and doated upon themselves in the Survey of his.

He was, as to his Proportion, middle-siz'd, inclinable to be fat, and of a gay jolly Complexion. His Manner of living, was imprinted in his Face, and none that saw him, but might have easily told his Profession, without making Application to *John Partridge*, *Isaac Bickerstaff*, or any other Astrologer in *Christendom*, for a Scheme to know it by. His Temper was of a Piece with his Person, daring and good-humour'd, if not provok'd, but insolent,

lent, uneafy, and unforgiving to the laft Degree, if at any Time impos'd upon. His Knowledge in Affairs relating to his Calling, was grounded upon a ftrong natural Judgment, and a fufficient Experience, that was highly advanc'd by an inceffant Application to the Mathematicks ; and notwithftanding the Remiffnefs of his Education and Converfe in his Minority, he had many Principles of Morality, which fince his Defection from an equitable Procedure, feveral of the Subjects belonging to the Crown of *Great Britain*, have fufficiently experienc'd.

Thefe Vertues, both natural and acquir'd, gain'd him a Reputation with the moft intelligent Perfons, that either apply'd themfelves to Navigation, or had Dealings with thofe that did ; and the moft accurate in their Projections, had an Eye upon him, as one that might advance

advance as far upon the Surface of the Ocean, and make as signal Discoveries, as his Predeceflors, the Admirals *Drake* and *Hawkins*, who had both, like him, been Inhabitants of *Plymouth*, and were rais'd from no higher Beginnings, than our modern Adventurer.

But *Fate* had decreed it otherwife, and he was juft upon the Point of feeing himfelf a Great Man by honeft Practices, when an unlucky Accident fhipwreck'd his good Fortune, and occafion'd his being enroli'd in the Lift of Robbers himfelf, who had not long fince been plunder'd of his Patrimony, by bafe and indirect Meafures.

It happen'd, that among other Paffions he was fubject to, that of Love was not the leaft; and he had pitch'd his Eyes upon a Farmer's Daughter, as one that would

make

make him happy in matrimonial Enjoyments after his Return from Sea, from which thofe Pleafures avert their Face; and as his Circumftances were as agreeable to the Parents, as his Appearance to the Daughter, the Portion was agreed upon, and they were both marry'd, (as every one thought) to their mutual and lafting Contentment.

Tho' it prov'd, that the Farmer was none of the honefteft, as his Daughter happen'd afterwards to fall under the Character of none of the chafteft; for the firft took Advantage of his Son-in-Law's taking his Word for his Daughter's Portion, and refus'd to pay him one Farthing, the laft was hopefully brought to bed of a champion Boy, fix Mouths after the Bridal Night, as much like a certain Inn-keeper in the Town, as if it had been fpit out of his Mouth.

'Tis

'Tis eafy to imagine fuch Difappointments as thefe, were enough to fet a Temper on Fire, that was too fanguine to pocket fuch Abufes; wherefore, having withdrawn his Effects from *Plymouth*, and made ready Money of all he was Mafter of, he made the beft of his Way for *London*, and gave a plain Indication, at his Arrival there, that as Hatred and Averfion make us bloody-minded, fo they teach us to diffemble; while he difguis'd his Thoughts, in order to put them more mifchievoufly in Execution.

Here he had no fooner made the proper Reflexions on his Misfortunes, and heartily curs'd the Authors of his Ruin, according to ancient Cuftom, but he put on very honeft undefigning Looks, and apply'd himfelf once more to fome Merchants, whofe Service he had been formerly engag'd in, and for whom he had made many a fuccefsful

ful Voyage. He pretended a more than ordinary Defire of repairing his Loffes by Trade; and to that Purpofe affur'd them, that he would not only venture all the ready Monies he was already poffefs'd of, but whatever Goods his Stock of Reputation could purchafe, after the unhappy Accidents that had befallen him: Which Propofals were readily clos'd with, and the Gentlemen apply'd to, not only fitted him out a Ship of 400 Tuns, ready mann'd, victall'd, and freighted, but gave him Credit for feveral hundred Pounds, and made him Supercargo, as well as Commander.

This was as he could have wifh'd, and the War between *England* and *France* raging at that Time, it afforded Capt. *Avery* a fair Opportunity of providing his Ship with a far greater Number of Guns and Men, than at any other Time would have appear'd neceffary. Neither did

did the Pains he took to procure able Sailors upon this Occasion, and such as were remarkable for their Courage, give any Manner of Suspicion to the Owners, but out he sail'd with as bold a Crew, as ever trusted themselves to Wind and Weather.

The Reader is not to expect, that he touch'd at *Plymouth*, to see his dear vertuous Wife, and his honest Promise-keeping Father-in-Law; for he had quite different Sentiments, and the Dishonours of a violated nuptial Bed, the Perjuries of a Guardian, and the Disregard shewn to sacred Agreements, made him loath having any other Commerce or Sight of Mankind, but such as launch'd out into the Deep with him, and such as he should for the future meet with, in order to be made Sacrifices to his Resentment and Ambition.

His

His firſt Exploit, after he had got Sea-room, was, to found the Inclination of his Men, for nothing was to be done without their Concurrence. "He laid before 'em the
"frequent Hazards they were ob-
"lig'd to run, for no valuable Con-
"ſideration: That if they would
"permit him to lead them on, he
"promis'd one Day's reſolute
"Fight ſhould make the Reſidue
"of their Lives an uninterrupted
"Scene of Pleaſure: That it was
"mere Madneſs to depend on the
"Merchants, who ſuffer'd the bra-
"veſt Fellows to grow old, lame,
"and miſerable in their Service,
"without having any Regard to
"their Labours: That 'twas an
"equal Frenzy, to hazard all for
"the Government, where, as he
"had perſonally experienc'd, Pro-
"motion ſeldom attended true
"Merit; where the Inſolence of
"Commanders was inſufferable,
"and where the Tarpawlins of
"Honour

"Honour had nothing to expect
"for the Reward of their Wounds
"and Bravery, but a poor Apart-
"ment in an unprovided Hospital,
"when Age and ill Usage had ren-
"der'd 'em unfit for farther Ser-
"vice.

With these, and such-like Arguments, drawn from the unfortunate Management of the Navy in those Days, and by perswading his Men, that they should meet with Mines richer than those of *Potosi*, he so far prevail'd with 'em, that, one and all, they determin'd to adhere to his Resolutions. Thus, being well satisfy'd with their Consent to his Design, he forthwith made the best of his Way to the Island of *Jamaica*, where he was not a little acquainted, (as the Reader has been before given to understand) and there dispos'd of that part of the Ship's Cargo which could be of no Use to him in his intended Voyage.

But

But an unlucky Accident had like to have marr'd his Project, and blasted a Design which he had conceiv'd so hopeful an Opinion of, for the Person whom he had chosen for his Clerk and Steward, being appriz'd of the Matter, and puff'd up with the Expectation of a great Reward for the Discovery, had made an Agreement with one of the Ship's Crew, who was the Gunner's Mate, to go ashore the next Day, and make it known to Sir *William Beeston*, who was then Governor; but the Fellow whom this Resolution was concerted with, had some Remorse amidst his Want of it, and communicated the whole Secret to the Captain, who laid an Embargo on his trusty Servant, 'till they were out at Sea, and then decently truss'd him up, for being a Traytor to his trayterous and piratical Purposes.

Being victuall'd afresh, he incited some Persons, who had been Buccaneers,

Buccaneers, to join him, and with all imaginable Expedition, set Sail to cruize in the *Indian* Sea; where, after an Oath taken of every individual Mariner, for Secrecy in the Affair they were going in Persuit of, he tack'd about backwards and forwards for a considerable Time, before any Prize of Value came in Sight. At last, *Fortune*, that intended to make him miserable, by being reputed happy, threw in his Way a Vessel of a great Burthen, for she carry'd near a thousand Men, with Guns proportionable, was freighted with the richest Merchandizes of all the *East*, and had got a Prize of greater Value about her, I mean a Grand-Daughter of *Aurenzebe*, who was then Great Mogul, and commanded an Empire almost as extensive as any known Quarter of the World.

The Force of the Ship, and the vast Numbers of Soldiers that appear'd on its Deck, at first gave no
small

small Uneasiness to Capt. *Avery*, who was loath to miscarry in his first Attempt, and seem'd doubtful of Success at the same Time as he was set on Tip-toe to prosecute it; but having recollected himself, he consider'd his own Strength, the Bravery of his Sea-men, and their wonderful Skill in naval Rencounters, while the Numbers of the others would rather be a Hinderance to 'em, than an Advantage, and the Want of being unexercis'd in military Affairs, render'd them as weak as they were numerous: Therefore he gave Orders for the Signal of Battel, and immediately commanded to bear down upon the *Indians*, and exerted such a Courage, as if he had prophetically known, that the Reward of his Victory should be the most charming of the fair Sex, and the most precious of all inestimable Things, that the *East* could present him with.

The *English* gave but a Broadside or two, when the *Indians* ſtruck their Colours, and reſign'd themſelves to the Mercy of their Enemies. The Cargo of this Ship was ſo very rich, that it even ſatiated the Appetites of the moſt covetous of the Mariners; for above the Value of a Million of Money in Silver, and rich Stuffs, was found therein, and a very agreeable Lady into the Bargain.

The Captain no ſooner beheld the Lady in Tears, but melted into Compaſſion, forgot thoſe inhuman Reſolutions he had taken at his Departure from *England*, and being of an amorous Diſpoſition, notwithſtanding his Wife had ſerv'd him the ſcurvy Trick before-mention'd, inſtead of raviſhing the Princeſs, which ſome Accounts have made Mention of, pay'd the Reſpect that was due to her high Birth, took her and her Attendance into his own Ship, and after deſpoiling

spoiling the Vessel of all its Wealth, suffer'd it and its Crew to steer on to their intended Port.

It seems the Riches of the Ship was design'd as a Portion for the Princess, and was sent as a Present to a *Persian* Potentate, who never had the Fortune to enjoy the glittering Cargo, nor his intended 'Spouse; for the Captain had plunder'd her of something more pleasing than the Jewels, though not without her own Consent, and being join'd in Marriage, after the Custom of those Foreigners, for she had a Priest with her, who did that Office after her Country's Manner; and *Avery* was e'en contented to dismiss the Scruples of his being marry'd after the Church of *England* Method, out of Complaisance to so desireable a Creature.

The rest of the Ship's Crew drew Lots for her Servants, and to follow the Example of their Commander, even stay'd their Stomachs 'till

'till the fame Prieſt had faid Grace for them that did it for their Maſter, when they fell to as heartily, as if they were to feaſt after that Rate no more during their Lives; and being full of Wealth, when they were almoſt empty of Love, came in Sight of the Iſland of *Madagaſcar*.

This Exploit of theirs having reach'd the Mogul's Ears in a ſhort Time after, he immediately caus'd three hundred thouſand Men to advance towards the *Engliſh* Settlements, by Way of Repriſals; but the *India*-Company being appriz'd of his Reſentments, ſtopt his Anger with Preſents, 'till they could give Notice to their Correſpondents in *England*, who bought Dr. D—*nt* a fine Gown to appear in as their Ambaſſador at the Mogul's Court; but the Doctor was either too fearful to venture his Carcaſs where it might not be ſafe, or too intent on a Place which he had in view at Home, to go

ſo

so far to seek for it Abroad, though Sir *William Norris* bravely accepted the Employment, and went thro' it with a Courage peculiar to his heroick Family.

The Mogul, at his Arrival into his Territories, not only defray'd his Charges, but sent him Home with rich Presents, though he had the Misfortune to die in his Return thither, and not bring 'em Home to his Family in Person; which shews, that a covetous Prince minds Money more than Consanguity, and makes the Maxim good, *That Princes have no Relations, while either the Extent of their Territories are concern'd, or the Augmentation of their Treasures.*

To return to *Madagascar*, where we left our triumphant Heroe and Lover, with the rest of his Adventurers. They were no sooner in Sight of the Island, but whole Troops of Inhabitants came down to the Shore, in order to take a
Survey

Survey of the Ship, and the People he brought with him. The Captain was somewhat ftartl'd at fo numerous an Appearance, but being told of the Fertility of the Ifland by fome of the Buccaneers, and the Difpofition of its Inhabitants, fent fome of 'em with a Flag of Truce, and Prefents for their chief Commanders, who no fooner receiv'd them, but with Expreffions of Joy after their Way, conducted 'em to their King.

Their Prince's Refidence was about three Miles off from the Shore, which was furrounded, after the manner of the *Eaftern* People, and made up of great Numbers of Huts. Here they found drawn up in a Semicircle about a thoufand arm'd Men, and in the Midft of 'em fat down on a Carpet crofs-legg'd three Perfons, who feem'd fuperior to the reft by their Habit and Looks. The Middlemoft was the Chief, and the other two

that

that fat at a convenient Diftance on each Side of him, his Brother, and Prime Minifter of State. The *Europeans* were no fooner come in Sight, but the little Army made a difmal Cry, and brandifh'd their Spears in the Air, in a feemingly threatning Pofture; which they underftood afterwards by Means of an Interpreter, was defign'd as a Welcome to Court. In an Inftant, all was Attention and Silence, and two or three Officers of State ftep'd out of their Ranks to conduct the Pirates to Audience; who, having paid their Refpects in their Country Manner, told him, " The " Occafion of their coming into " thofe Parts, was for the Wealth, " and Advantage of the Country; " that their Commander was a ve- " ry powerful and great Man, and " having receiv'd fome Injuries " from the Potentates of *Europe*, " was in Search of a Place conve- " nient, from whence he might " moleft

"moleft 'em in the moft fenfible "Part, which was, that of Trade; "and that his Arrival in thofe "Parts, would not only make "him a Prince formidable to his "Neighbours, but all the World "would come into an Alliance "with their Mafter, and defire to "make Settlements in his Terri- "tories. His Majefty, after having been told, by his chief Minifter, the Purport of their Errand, gave them to underftand, that an Alliance with fo great a Commander, would be very welcome; and that he himfelf would, after due Preparations for his Reception, go in Perfon and attend him to Court; and having given Orders for their Entertainment, and fhewn his great Satisfaction in the Prefent, which were but Trifles, rofe up, and retir'd, as is ufual with the Oriental Princes, to converfe with his Wives.

In the mean Time, Capt. *Avery*, to lofe no Time, fet all Hands at work

work in founding the Bay of the *East* side of this Island, in 15 Degrees 30 Minutes *South* Latitude, which was large and capacious, and unexpos'd to the Fury of the most tempestuous Weather. Towards the bottom of it, lies a small Island, about ten Miles in Circumference, whose Land round it being high and woody, makes it a sure Protection for all Vessels which anchor'd beneath; and here he chose to continue 'till the Return of his Messengers, who made him the Report above-mention'd.

The King of the Country was as good as his Word in a Day or two after, and came very nobly attended to invite the Captain ashore, who receiv'd him under a Discharge of all his Artillery, and with all the Respect due to a Person of the highest Character; and having entertain'd him and his Retinue with all Things the Ship afforded, which was of an astonishing Bulk to the Infidels,

Infidels, very frankly accepted of his Invitation, and went afhore, where he found a Treatment that was uncommon with *Barbarians,* and made him affur'd, that he was not the only *European* that had touch'd upon thofe Ports.

Here the two Potentates (for we muft, after this Interview, fhare the Government of this fide of the World between them) enter'd into a perpetual Alliance, and having regal'd themfelves after an extraordinary manner, ftipulated to ftand by each other with all their Forces; when the Captain return'd to his Ship, in order to take Poffeffion of the Place which was intended for his Aboad, and was the Ifland we juft now told the Reader of, and on which, after mooring his Veffel, he landed with all his Crew, but fuch as were abfolutely neceffary to look after her.

In the firft place, what he had to do, was, to caufe all the Plunder he he had got, to be brought aſhore, and take Care that an exact Dividend ſhould be made of the whole, according to the Law of Pirates, who, though they make it their Buſineſs to prey on Perſons of a different Life and Converſation, yet among themſelves obſerve the ſtricteſt Rules of Juſtice.

He had no ſooner diſpos'd of his Affairs, to the general Satisfaction, cur'd his ſick Men, and careen'd his Veſſel, but he embark'd again, having left part of his Crew, with the Women, aſhore, to look after freſh Booty, and ſet Sail for the neighbouring Iſles, which lay contiguous and interſpers'd in thoſe Seas, not far from one another; ſome of which were of dangerous Acceſs, others afforded convenient Harbours, but all of 'em in general were found to abound with moſt Neceſſaries of Life, as what were wanting ſeem'd rather deſign'd to oblige the Luxurious, than to anfwer the Demands of a reasonable Appetite.

During this Cruize, in which he took two *Moorish* Vessels, and an *English East India* Ship outward bound, and very richly laden, he had Time to consider of his past Life and Conduct, and consult with himself for his future Safety. He debated what Course was most proper for him to take: To return into *England*, was dangerous; all the World were his Enemies, and if he escap'd the Danger of the Seas on such a Voyage, he had Reason to believe he should perish at Land. These Reasons induc'd him to be fix'd in his Resolves, to chuse the Place he had left the Women and Plunder in, for a Retreat, since none could be more proper than those very Isles about which he was then cruizing, their Scituation for Trade lying as it were between the *East* and *West Indian* Seas.

Their

Their Neighbourhood to several Spice Iflands, the Civility of their Inhabitants, their Diftance from *Europe*, and the Plenty of Provifions that were found therein, powerfully induc'd him to fettle here a Colony, which feem'd to be fecure enough from all the Attempts that the Univerfe could make againft it. Refolv'd upon this *Medium*, to avoid future Dangers, after having taken another Prize, which was full of *French*-Men, defign'd for the fame Exploits which he was then in the Exercife of, he communicated his Thoughts not only to his Ship's Crew, but fuch of his Prifoners as were *Englifh* or *French*; and at the fame Time affur'd them, that fuch who diflik'd his Propofal, were at Liberty to retire aboard one of the Ships which he would furnifh them with.

The Captain's Generofity was fo very much applauded, that very few, either *Englifh* or *French*, except the Commanders of the *East India* Ship, and part of his Crew, made the laſt Offer their Choice. The *French*, for their parts, being ſenſible that they were one and all in his Power, thought it rather Prudence to ſhare his Fortune, than for him to make himſelf Maſter of theirs, and more than ſupply'd the Room of thoſe Sailors that were for returning into their own Countries, tho' moſt of the *Engliſh* tarry'd with their Commander, and landed with all Materials neceſſary to build a Fort with, for their mutual Defence.

This they effected in a little Time, and having plac'd ſeveral great Guns upon it, and forty eight Pieces of Cannon they had taken out of the *Eaſt India* Ship, for the Security of their Perſons and Effects, and call'd it by the Name of *Fort Avery*, in Honour of their Leader, but as Bulwarks and Artillery were not able to preſerve
this

this piratical Government, without Laws and Inftitutions neceffary for its Well-being and Continuance, feveral new Cuftoms and Ordinances were propos'd, and confented to by the Generality of the Rovers, conducive as they imagin'd neceffary for the Prefervation of their new State; and *Avery* was with abundance of Ceremony chofen and confirm'd in the Dignity of being their Chief, with fuch a Power as the Doges or Dukes of *Venice* and *Genoa* are now poffefs'd of.

After this Republick of Pirates had thus order'd all Things to their Satisfaction, thofe who had Leave to retire, were fhipp'd for the *Weftern* Iflands in one of the *Moorifh* Veffels, and part of *Avery*'s new Subjects remain'd upon the Ifland, while the other weigh'd Anchor from thence, in Search of new Adventures, under the Command of Monfieur *de Sale*, who was next in Power to the new Duke, who, for

his

his part, with his other Companions, who had Women for their Shares, gave himself up to the Careſſes of his new Princeſs.

As Time obliterates the moſt deep Impreſſions of Sorrow, ſo the Lady was not long before ſhe forgot the Pleaſures of her Grand-father's Court, in the Joys of her own, and found her ſelf happily brought to Bed of a Son ſoon after her Huſband's being inveſted with her new Dignity, while the Female part of her Retinue were no leſs backward in preſenting their Huſbands with the Fruits of their conjugal Endearments. But tho' the Commander in Chief, with a ſmall Number of his Followers, had theſe Advantages, the reſt of 'em were Strangers to Venereal Enjoyments, and being Maſters of the ſame Paſſions, were under a Reſtraint of being Strangers to the ſame Priviledges; wherefore it was reſolv'd, *nemine contradicente,* that a Supply ſhould be be granted, for the Good of their new-modell'd Government, and the firſt Voyage ſhould be made in Queſt of Women, to perpetuate it by way of Generation, leſt the Want of Aſſiſtants from that Sex, ſhould, in Procefs of Time, render it extinct by a Failure of Succeſſion.

Nor was *Fortune* averſe to their Deſires, the Ship ſoon return'd with a Cargo of Ladies. 'Tis true, their Complexion was none of the faireſt, but *Neceſſity* takes up with every Thing; and when they were weary of theſe, 'twas in their Power to have more at the ſame Price, it being the Cuſtom of the Iſlands, and of that part of the Continent of *Africa* which lay near, to barter for Wives as they do for Cattel, and you might as eaſily purchaſe a young Virgin of her Parents, as a Tooth of Ivory, both being the Commodities and Merchandize of thoſe Countries, only here lay the Difference,

Difference, the Lady was of lefs Value than the Tooth.

Thus Capt. *Avery* and his Adherence, meeting with all they could in Reafon defire in that part of the World where they liv'd, refolv'd to make their conftant Refidence, and by Force or Perfwafion, oblige feveral *Europeans* to partake in the Fortunes of their new-ftructur'd Commonwealth ; and in a little Time *Fame* fo aſſifted their Intentions, that feveral Pirates of all Nations came to fettle themfelves under his Protection, and he faw himfelf in Poffeffion of a Government larger than he could have imagin'd in the Infancy of his Adventures.

By this Acceffion of Strength, he not only enlarg'd his Territories, but made all the neighbouring Princes his Tributaries. Towns were built, Communities eftablifh'd, Fortifications built, and Entrenchments flung up, as render'd his Dominions

minions impregnable and inaccessible by Sea and Land; and tho' Commadore *Warren* came into those Parts with a Squadron of Men of War, to drive 'em from thence, he had the Mortification to see such Efforts not only hazardous, but impracticable, and to return Home without any other Effect, than dispersing a Pardon, which was embrac'd by few of the Captain's Adherents, because their Commander in Chief was excepted.

But as in all Constitutions and Bodies Politick, there are still some Members that compose it, of different Inclinations, and who, sway'd by Ambition, or byass'd by Disaffection, think themselves capable of commanding the whole, and highly injur'd while they are made subservient to a Power that is superior to 'em; so it was with *de Sale*, who, not being content to be second, lost his Life, with his Expectations, while he was attempting to be first. This

This Man was a brave and daring Officer, but not being content that *Avery* had not only fpar'd his Life, when he firſt made him his Prifoner, but alſo advanc'd him to be his Vice-roy, as it were, and the next in Command under him, he refolv'd to return thoſe Acts of Mercy and Compaſſion, with the higheſt Injuſtice and Cruelty.

The Lady that fell to his Share for a Help-mate, was neither beautiful, like Capt. *Avery*'s, nor of high Extraction, and he could not caſt an Eye on the one, without having the utmoſt Averſion for the other. He made uſe of all the little Artifices he could, to make the other's Lady acquainted with his Paſſion, but either ſhe had too much Generoſity for her Huſband's Friend and Deputy, or too little Knowledge in the Art and Myſteries of Love, to be ſenſible of his Deſigns, without a more formal Declaration: Whether it was Ignorance

norance of Addreſs in her, it is nothing to
our Purpoſe ; the more innocent ſhe appear'd to the *French*-Man, ſhe ſeem'd ſtill
Miſtreſs of the more Charms ; and he took
Reſolutions to enjoy her, that were as Fatal as his Love was criminal.

The Captain's Abſence from the Place
of his uſual Abode, on the Affairs of his
Government, gave the Villain an Opportunity of being more ſedulous in his Addreſſes, and he laid hold of it with an Ea-
gerneſs that ſhew'd how impatient he was
of any Delay, as he took *Time* by the Fore-
lock in the following manner. As the Violence of his Paſſion had made him reſolute and intrepid, ſo the Deſpair of ſucceeding in his Amours by fair Means, made
him wholly intent how to accompliſh his
Deſires by foul, whatſoever ſhould be the
Conſequence : But firſt he thought it a
piece of Diſcretion, to feel the Pulſe of his
Country-Men the *French*, to whom he addreſs'd himſelf by way of Complaint, relating to "the Tyranny of the *Engliſh*,
" who would Lord it over 'em in a ſtrange
" manner, unleſs Methods were ſpeedily
" apply'd, to prevent their exorbitant In-
" creaſe of Power. He told them, that it
" was but too viſible to thoſe who would
" make any Enquiry into his paſt and pre-
" ſent Conduct, that *Avery* aim'd at a de-
" ſpotical and arbitrary Government :
" That ſuch Deſigns were deſtructive of
" the very Being of their Settlement : That
it

" it behov'd every well-meaning Perſon, eſ-
" pecially thoſe of the *French* Nation, who
" had been ſo long us'd to Conqueſts, to
" ſhake off a Yoke that would never be
" got rid of, without their immediate ta-
" king Advantage of the Captain's Abſence:
" That it was their Turn to re'ieve the
" Guard, and do Duty at the Caſtle that
" Day, and they at this very Juncture not
" only had it in their Power to deliver
" themſelves from approaching Slavery, but
" making Terms with their Prince, whom
" they had highly offended by tranſgreſſing
" the Law of Nations, in taking ſuch un-
" lawful Courſes as they were forc'd to un-
" der their preſent Circumſtances: That
" all the Riches of *Avery*, which were in-
" conceivably great, were lodg'd in the
" Caſtle they were going to be poſſeſs'd of,
" and that beſides thoſe Riches, they might
" have immenſe Treaſures from the Mogul,
" in reſcuing his Grand-daughter, the
" Princeſs, from her unjuſt Confinement,
" and delivering her into his Hands, which
" might be done by a due Capitulation.
" To conclude, he conjur'd 'em, by the
" Honour of their Country, and the Re-
" ſpect they bore to him, their Comman-
" der, who had journey'd ſo many thou-
" ſand Leagues with 'em, to ſhew them-
" ſelves Men, in order to be poſſeſs'd of ſo
" glorious a Reward; and for his part, he
" would not only lead 'em on, but would
" be the laſt that ſhould ſee 'em on Board
" their

"their own Vessel again, in their Return
"Home, after the Prosecution of so noble
"and equitable a Design.

The Prospect of Gain, the Hopes of having their Pardons, and the Return to their native Soil, were Arguments too perswasive not to make Impressions upon the Minds of Men, who, being accustom'd to the Acts of Barbarity, made no Scruple of falling into Measures that were consonant to it; wherefore they jointly, one and all, agreed to live and die with their Commander, and as soon as the Watch-Bell should found, after their being possess'd of the Castle, to fall to, and plunder all they should find in their Way, and neither spare Man, Woman, or Child, but the Princess and her Family.

But here, as before at *Jamaica*, Capt. *Avery*'s good Genius was superior to his evil, and stood by him once more, in Opposition to his Enemies, though perhaps to reserve him for greater Misfortunes, if he persists in the Course of Life he yet continues to take. One *Pickard*, of *de Sale*'s Crew, had been very much abus'd by him, bastinado'd, and under an Arrest frequently when on Board with him, besides incapable of returning to *France* again for other Crimes, as Murder and Incest, should that of Piracy be forgiven him; wherefore, after having long sought for an Opportunity of Revenge, he could not but hug himself at the Thoughts of this, as an infallible

Means

Means to dispatch his Enemy. What does he therefore do, but makes off to the Captain of the Guard, one *Richardson*, a *Cornish*-Man, and formerly *Avery*'s Lieutenant, and acquaints him with the intended Conspiracy, giving him to understand, that unless he took speedy Measures to prevent it, two Hours Time would bring about such a Turn of Affairs as would be the unavoidable Ruin of their whole Colony. *Richardson*, for his part, was a prudent Man, and wisely entertain'd a true Sense of the Danger which his Master's Affairs were going to be involv'd in; wherefore, the first Thing he did, was, to dispatch a Messenger to Capt. *Avery*, with an Account of the Premises, and to desire his speedy Return, promising not only to secure his pernicious Deputy, but not to admit any Forces to relieve the Guard in the Castle.

All this was punctually perform'd, for *de Sale* coming, as his usual Custom was, to pay his Respects to the Princess about an Hour before the Guard was to be reliev'd, was immediately put under an Arrest, to his great Confusion. But as it was not enough to make a Seizure of his Person, without those of his Accomplices, so he was to look out for Measures suitable to this End, which was happily accomplish'd by his calling in a whole Ship's Crew of *English*, who were just come into Port with fresh Booty.

These

These he dispos'd in such a manner with those which he had before in Garrison, so as when the Relief should come upon the Parade, to surround 'em on every side, and either make 'em Prisoners, or cut 'em entirely off; out as Villains, never so desperate in their horrid Contrivances, have a cowardly Disposition of Soul when they come to Action, so these, when they saw themselves encompass'd, and commanded to lay down their Arms, or expect no Quarter, made Choice to submit to the Laws of *Necessity*, and were hurry'd to Prison without any manner of Resistance, where they are to stay 'till the Captain's and his Council's Arrival, who were to pass Sentence upon 'em answerable to their Demerits.

This was no sooner done, but the News of it spread over the whole Island, and not a *French*-Man could be seen in it, but was in Danger of his Life from the Indignation those of other Nations had conceiv'd against 'em; and had it not been for an Order that was issu'd out upon *Avery*'s Arrival, to prevent such inconsiderate and cruel Proceedings, they had found themselves wholly extinct by a general Massacre.

But Forms of Justice were to be made use of even among those People, whose way of Living shew'd 'em conversant with nothing but Injustice; and *de Sale* and his Accomplices were brought upon their Tryals, where, being found guilty, they were every Man condemn'd to be empal'd alive, and their Estates confiscated for the Use of the Government: Which severe Execution was accordingly put in Practice, without any Remorse on the side of the unhappy Persons, that while they were made the Objects of other Folks Terror, shew'd no other Concern under their Sufferings, than for their Villanies not being prosperous.

As Plots are for the Use and Confirmation of Governments, when unsuccessful, so was this highly to the Advantage of the Captain and his new Dignity, for not only vast Riches fell to him by the Forfeiture of these Conspirators, but the great Council of the Island agreed, one and all, to pass such wholesome Acts in his Favour, as rais'd him to a Pitch of Sovereignty not any ways inferior to the Greatest Potentates.

'Twas not only made high Treason to contrive against his Person, but to speak little of his Authority; and he saw himself invested with a Power as despotick as one of the most arbitrary Principles could wish for, or the highest Ambition could have in View. But as, amidst all the Prosperities of Life, Reflexions on the short Duration of 't will sometimes intervene, and the Inclinations of Mankind are not so sunk in Vice, as to admit no Thoughts that border upon Vertue, so the Captain could not but lean after a Prospect of his own native Country, and the Desire of

finishing

finishing the Remainder of his Days where he first had the Happiness of seeing the Light, which was increas'd by looking into his past Crimes, and a just Survey of what he must one Day answer for at a Heavenly Tribunal, tho' he found himself out of the Reach of one that was Earthly.

These Considerations, which he found himself more and more subject to, induc'd him to make Application to the *English* Company trading to the *East Indies*, for Pardon; and having an Opportunity by one of their Ships, which was then brought in, and which he order'd to be immediately releas'd with great Civilities, he wrote the following Letter to Capt. *Pitts*, the Governor of *Fort St. George*.

SIR,

"THE Bearer can testify my Respects to the Company, by bringing you this; and whatever my Demeanor has been to other Nations, you may always rest assur'd of my particular Deference to my own. Nothing lies more at Heart on my side, than that I have given Occasion for her Majesty's Subjects formerly to complain of me; but as I have it in my Power to make ample Amends, so I am now ready to do it, after what manner shall be thought convenient; provided I may be suffer'd to return Home to my own Country in Safety, with such Effects as shall be thought needful. The Necessities of the War, in all Probability, may

"may make a Proposal of some Millions
"of Money, not altogether unacceptable:
"And tho' I am capable of maintaining
"my self where I am, against whatsoever
"Power can be brought against me, yet
"my Distrelish of Things that are unjust,
"and my Inclination to do my own
"Country Service, as well as close my
"Eyes in it, are so prevalent with me, as
"to make me desire your good Offices in
"this Affair, and tell you, that I am,
"with all imaginable Respect. Sir,
 "Your most obedient Servant,
  "*John Avery.*

This Letter, according to Request, was transmitted into *England*, but whether the *East India* Company thought it not adviseable to be presented to the Government, or the Ministry took no Notice of it, as an Affair too despicable, and directly coming to Terms with a Pirate and Rebel, as well as Violator of the Laws of Nations, it is not in my Power to determine; for he had no manner of Answer to it, and was left to take such Measures as he should think most conducive to his present Circumstances, which were such as not to render him contemptible.

But to return to *Madagascar*, without making Enquiry into our Transactions at Home. This remarkable Deliverance of the Captain from the Machinations of his Enemies, not only gave Being to a Law, That all *French*-Men whatsoever should depart

part that Island, but occasion'd Resolutions in *Avery* and his Council, to persue 'em to Death wheresoever they should find 'em. And accordingly a Fleet was equipp'd to obstruct their Commerce, and destroy their Settlements in the *North* part of that Island; which was effected with that Vigor and Celerity, that all the Resistance could be made by the Enemy, could not withstand 'em; and they return'd from *Port St. Mary* (for that was the chief Place the *French East India* Company had been in Possession of ever since the Year 1664) with upwards of two Millions in Plate, Jewels, and other valuable Commodities; a fourth-Part of which fell to the Captain's Share, according to the Constitution of his Government.

Thus he grew in Wealth, as he grew in Years, and scarce a Week pass'd without some new adventitious Booty; so that if Money could purchase his Pardon and safe Return, he had wherewithal to reduce *France*, notwithstanding their coining their Plate, without any farther Taxes upon the Subject; and he had nothing short of the Regal Authority, but a Right to exercise it: For the Fame of his Adventures had brought all manner of People to live under his Government; and he not only coin'd Money with his own Impress upon it, but took upon him the Stile, in his Edicts and Declarations, that is to be made use of by Sovereign Princes. And he not only beat

the

The *French* out of their Dominions in that Island, but, to gratify his Ambition by not having any Thing like a Competitor, wag'd War with the King of the Country, that so handsomely receiv'd him at his first coming to it, and having reduc'd him, makes him now live under the Denomination of a Subject.

But as has been said before, all Governments are insecure, that are founded upon Violence and Rapine, and tho' he had been preserv'd from the Attempts of his pretended Friends, he had all imaginable Reason to make use of Means to defend himself from his open and avow'd Enemies; nor was he such a Stranger to the Affairs of *Europe*, how remote soever he was from the Confines of it, not to foresee that Attempts would be made to dislodge him from thence on every side, at the Conclusion of a general Peace: He therefore set himself at work to regulate, arm, and discipline his Militia, and having form'd them into several Regiments, found them to make fifteen thousand effective Men.

His Preparations at Sea were nothing behind those at Land, and he saw himself Master of more than forty Vessels of War, from twenty to thirty six Guns, that could be laid up on Occasion in a Bason that was defended by a Mole and a hundred Pieces of Cannon.

The Forts were likewise kept in Repair, and such additional Works added to em, as might defeat all the Measures should be taken against him, and every Thing was put into such a Posture, as not only enabled him to repel Force by Force, but defy'd the Approach of an Enemy within Reach of 'em.

To go farther than this, would be to impose upon the Veracity of the Relators, as well as the Belief of the Reader, because the Person that gives him these Memoirs, left the Captain when he first made Overtures for Pardon; wherefore we shall release him from any farther Enquiries, by a faithful and true Account of the Country which he is now possess'd of, and which he may take as follows.

MADAGASCAR, or *St. Lawrence's* Island, so call'd because discover'd on that Day; and, according to some, from *Lawrence*, a *Portuguese*, who discover'd it in 1506. The *French*, in the Reign of *Henry* the IVth, call'd it the *Dauphine's* Island. It is suppos'd to be the *Menuthias* of *Ptolomy*, and the *Cerne-Æthiopia* of *Pliny*. It lies in the *Æthiopian* Sea, and points Westward towards *Zanguebar* and the *Cafres*, on the Coast of *Africk*. Tis about 50 Leagues in Length, and 80 or 100 in Breadth. It is under the *Torrid Zone*, and the *Tropick* of *Capricorn*. It hath abundance of Capes, and most of them cover'd with Citron and Orange, or Ebeny-Trees, and others, whose Wood is speckl'd. The
Rocks

Rocks are of excellent white Marble, whence flows the best and purest Water in the World. The Country is divided into many Provinces; but those towards the *North*, are unknown to the *Europeans*. Their Villages are compos'd of moveable Houses, such as four Men can carry. Their Towns are encompass'd with Pales, and a deep Ditch six or seven Foot wide, and their Houses built of Planks. The Air is extream hot, and they have never any Snow nor Ice.

Here are several Mines of Iron and fine Steel. They have some Mines of Gold, but it is very pale. Most Sorts of precious Stones are to be found in their Rivers; and they have Store of excellent Honey, sweeter and harder than ours, resembling Sugar. They make Wine or Mead of Honey, which is the most common; Wine of Sugar, and a Sort of Cyder. They extract Oil from several Plants, Fruits, Nuts, and Grains, and have a Sort of Earth as good as the *Terra Sigillata* of *Limnos*.

- Here grows abundance of white Pepper, and precious odoriferous Wood of divers Colours. They have also Store of Canes of a vast Height and Thickness, tall and round, of which they make Pots, Bottles, Violins, and Harps, Boats that will hold two Persons, and Sedans, and take Care to give them a certain Bent, when young, to render 'em fit for their Purpose. These Canes, which they call *Bambuches*, have a

Pith

Pith within, much esteem'd by the *Indians*, *Arabians*, and *Persians*, and call'd the Sugar of the *Bamba's*, or *Bambuches*.

They have a very good Tobacco; and also a Sort of Hemp; whose Leaves they use instead of it, which being chew'd, makes them fall asleep, and afterwards renders them extraordinary chearful; but such as are not accustom'd to it, it makes mad for three or four Days. The Inhabitants are often incommoded with Locusts, which destroy all their Corn and Fruits; but the Natives gather up the Locusts, and feed upon them. Here are no great Plenty of noisome Animals, except Crocadiles, and great Serpents without Poison.

The Natives are of two Sorts, black and white; the latter, by their Names and Customs, seem to be of *Jewish* Extract. All of 'em go naked, but cover their *Pudenda*. Women of Quality have some slight Habit extraordinary. The Men buy their Wives, and keep as many as they can maintain. The Men are courageous and despise Death; and their Arms are Javelins, Bows and Arrows. The Women are very discreet, and extreamly virtuous. Their Language and Writing resembles the *Arabick*. Their Paper is yellow, very smooth, and fine, being made of the inner Rind of a certain Tree, call'd *Avo*. Their Ink is a sort of Gum, made of a Tree call'd *Arandranto*, and their Pens made of Cane. They believe in one God, the Creator of Heaven and Earth, who rewards the Good, and punishes the Bad: They call him *Zankarre*, and sacrifice to him, but without Temples. They own also, that there are good and evil Angels, and are mightily afraid of the Devil; and in all their Sacrifices, they throw the Devil the first Bit, to pacify him. Their Priests are usually Magicians, and give 'em Spells and Charms to prevent Mischief from the Devil. They live in Hords, like the *Tartars*, under one Chief, whom they call *Tschich*: Which Authority is many times usurp'd by him who is most powerful. The latest Relation from this Island, informs us, that the Princes are govern'd by petty Princes or Grandees, and the People are divided into several Ranks; tho' all these Princes, since the Reduction of the Island by Capt. *Avery*, are under his Obedience. When the Grandees visit one another, he who receives the Visit, prostitutes his handsomest Wife to the other: And the common People entertain their Friends and Strangers in the same Manner. Their Grandees are much delighted with Comedies. Their Comedians, whom they call *Secalses*, shave themselves close, and act in the Habit of Women, and play their Part in a Farce divertingly enough.

The Air here is generally very temperate, and exceeding wholsome. The opposite Place on the Globe to *Madagascar*, is, the South Part of *California*. The Soil is extraordinary fruitful, in many places affording all Things neceſſary for the Life of Man in great Plenty. The longeſt Day in the *North* Parts, is about 13 Hours and half, and the ſhorteſt in the *South* 9 Hours and three quarters, and the Nights proportionably.

The chiefeſt Commodities of this Place, are, Rice, Hides, Wax, Gums, Chriſtal, Steel, Copper, Ebony, and Wood of all ſorts. Towards the *Eaſtern* Part of this Iſland, is a pleaſant and fertil Valley, call'd *Ambouſe*, which is ſtock'd with ſeveral rich Mines of Iron and Steel, and yields great Store of the Oil of *Sejanum*. Near to the ſame Valley, is an excellent Medicinal Well of hot Water, which proves a ready Cure for cold Diſtempers in the Limbs. In the ſame Neighbourhood, is an high Mountain, on whoſe Top is a remarkable Spring of very ſalt Water, tho' upwards of thirty Leagues from the Sea. In the *Southern* Parts are moſt ſorts of Mineral Waters, very different both in Colour, Taſte, and Quality, and ſome Places afford large Pits of *Bitumen*. In this Iſland is alſo a River, whoſe Gravel is ſo exceeding hot, that there's no treading upon it, and yet the Water of that River is extream cold.

Divers ſingular Cuſtoms prevail in ſeveral Parts of this Iſland, particularly theſe two; firſt, if any Woman be deliver'd of a live Child, and afterwards die in Childbed, the living Child is bury'd with the dead Mother, being better (ſay they) that the Child ſhould die, than live, having no Mother

Mother to look after it. The other is, their expofing their Children to wild Beafts, if brought forth upon an unlucky Day, (as they term it) or during fome unfortunate Afpects of the Planets, as their Priefts pretend to tell them; and fo numerous are thofe Days they term *unlucky*, that almoft one half of the Year is accounted fuch; which is the Reafon the Ifland is fo thinly ftock'd with Inhabitants.

The Language here us'd, is barbarous; almoft every Province has its peculiar Dialect, yet not fo different, but that they underftand one another; fo that the Natives of this Ifland may be faid to have but one Tongue in common among 'em all.

From the foregoing Defcription, may be concluded what a mighty Advantage it would be to the Crown of *Great Britain*, if Means could be found out by our Superiors, either to fupprefs thefe Pirates by Force, and fo get Poffeffion of this wealthy Ifland, or by Compliance with fuch Advances as have been made by their Chief towards his Pardon, which muft terminate in an entire Surrendry of a Country that not only abounds with fo many ufeful Commodities, but, by its Extent and Strength, will add to the Renown of the *Britifh* Arms, which, from fuch an Accommodation, muft fhine with as great a Luftre in *Africa*, as they have lately done in *Europe*.

FINIS.